A MURDER OF LIES

A DCI GARRICK THRILLER - BOOK 7

M.G. COLE

A MURDER OF LIES
A DCI Garrick mystery - Book 7

Copyright © 2023 by Max Cole (M.G.Cole)

Cover art: Shutterstock

MURDER OF
LIES

1

1

THE DULL, constant rumble was hypnotic. A soothing call into the arms of slumber. With little effort, he could let himself go. But it would be a fleeting moment of victory. A sleep that would be plagued by intense visions that seamlessly fused nightmare and reality, and exploited the senses, shattering the line between fiction and reality.

And they were getting worse.

David Garrick glanced across at Molly Meyers next to him. She was fast asleep and had been for the last couple of hours. Her TV screen was midway through a film he didn't recognise, and her seat was reclined, raising her feet, but that's all he could see of her in the small pod. They were travelling business class – a treat Molly had squeezed from the ordinarily frugal BBC current affairs producers. It was a first for Garrick, and the spacious pod seating allowed them privacy, aided by a screen between them that Molly had drawn across. Their seats ran down the centre of the fuselage, so he didn't have the luxury of a window view. Other windows around him had been darkened by sleeping passengers on the eight-hour four-five-minute journey from London Heathrow to Chicago O'Hare, robbing him of even glimpsing a view from forty-thousand feet. It was the longest single trip Garrick had ever taken and instead of enjoying the experience he was restless.

The dim cabin lighting didn't improve his mood. It cast everybody in shadows and added to a gnawing sense of claustrophobia – an affliction he rarely suffered, and only once when he had taken scuba diving lessons in University, in the ambitious hope of acquiring his PADI licence. He'd tried to distract himself. The United Airlines entertainment offered a broad range of films and TV shows, none of which he could watch for more than ten minutes before his mind wandered. Instead, he navigated through the touchscreen and settled on the inflight map. They were currently over Greenland, and he could only speculate on what bleak views he was missing out on below.

They'd left early in the morning, UK time, but because of the time difference, they would arrive before lunch in Chicago and Molly warned him they then had a long drive ahead, so advised him to rest as much as possible.

But every time he tried, his dead sister Emilie would make her presence known to him.

For the first time in a long time, Garrick had taken holiday leave from the force when reporter Molly Meyers had offered to fly him over to the States to record a BBC news special into the so-called Murder Club. It was a murky network of sick-minded serial killers, working together to unleash their perverse passions. Their roots had reached into the police force and even threatened to corrupt White Hall, but no connections there had yet been found. The single originator was narrowed down to John Howard, an ex-Falklands War vet, who had been a friend to Garrick.

Driven by motivations beyond David Garrick's comprehension, John Howard had followed his sister and her fiancé, Sam McKinzie, on their road trip around the US. It was supposed to be their last extravagant fling before they married and settled down. During the end of the holiday, they'd got stranded in a snowstorm just outside of Flora in Country Clay, Illinois. Evidence suggested that they found their way to a ranch, but from their details and motivations from the investigation were hazy, but it resulted in Sam being brutally murdered. It seemed Emilie had seized on the chance of escape – which involved sawing off two of her fingers which had trapped in a doorway. Even this desperate act of self-preservation was not enough. Her killers caught up with her, although her body was never retrieved.

It took some months before traces of her blood were found in the back of a car abandoned on a quiet country road in New York state. The cross-border nature of the crime moved it from a local police jurisdiction to that of the FBI. Garrick had developed a cordial relationship with the Flora Police Department, and the Sergeant who had been leading the investigation, although information was still difficult to squeeze out of the taciturn cop. He'd wavered between thinking them professional, respecting the security of their investigation, to inept because of their lack of progress. The moment the case was handed over to the FBI, the thin stream of information abruptly stopped. Even as the architect who revealed the Murder Club, the Feds had not tried to contact him, and the investigation in the UK was eventually taken out of his hands by the London based Metropolitan Police Force.

Molly Meyers had made her career on the back of DCI Garrick's high-profile cases, and her exclusives about the Murder Club had catapulted her journalistic credentials. Making the definitive investigational report on the Murder Club wouldn't do her any harm, either. While Garrick had refused to appear on camera, he couldn't resist the opportunity to poke around the crime scene himself.

Restless, he rose from his seat. He'd been drinking far too many complimentary cokes. He felt lightheaded due to low tolerance of the caffeine and the cabin pressure. It had made trips to the small forward toilet an essential regular occurrence.

The aircraft shuddered as it hit an air pocket, forcing Garrick to steady himself against the overhead luggage bins to stop himself from pitching into a stranger's lap. He wasn't a nervous flyer, but that didn't stop him from hating turbulence. During take-off, he focused on the lyrics to *Hotel California* to distract him from the menagerie of metallic noises the aircraft insisted on making as they soared into the air. That was followed by a nervous moment when the engines sounded as if they were powering down. He was sure Molly had noticed his panic, but she'd tactfully remained silent.

Luckily, the toilet cubical was vacant. The interior light came on as he entered and slid the bolt across the door. Using one hand to brace himself against the bulkhead, he relieved himself as the plane shuddered. Now he was more focused on no peeing down his leg as the jolt gently rocked the top of his head against the sloping ceiling. He lowered the lid but didn't flush. He would wait until he was leaving, as he couldn't ignore the urban legends that claimed passengers had been sucked down the loo in tragic accidents. It was a tight squeeze to turn around to face the sink so he could wash his hands in the trickle of cold water. The light above the mirror flickered as the plane trembled again.

And it happened again.

The lighting altered his face until he was staring into the eyes of his sister. It was his reflection, his clothing, but her doe-like eyes peered back. The first dozen times had been terrifying. The image was vivid, not a ghostly hallucination. It had occurred so often that by now he took it in his stride. It had been nothing more than an aberration since the doctors discovered a tumour pressing against his brain and triggering realistic visions.

He'd seen Emilie several times since she had died. Looming over him as he was wheeled into surgery, as a figure following him or moving just out of sight around the house. He had been assured that it was a common side effect due to pressure on the brain and the trauma of losing his sister.

CTE: Chronic traumatic encephalopathy.

In some, it triggered more violent reactions, especially in those who had suffered head trauma, such as professional athletes. The case of Kevin Tolson had stuck with him when he'd researched his condition. It was the usual story of the internet bringing the worst to the surface. Tolson was a former American Football player who'd gone on a random killing spree, slaying five people – including two children –

before taking his own life. CTE, caused by numerous head impacts on the football field, was eventually blamed.

Garrick had been thankful that his surgery had been successful. With the tumour removed, the swelling on his brain had stopped. As did the visions.

But now they were coming back. Perhaps triggered by the paranoia that Emilie had been targeted as an apparent 'experiment' see how Garrick would react. Before his death, John Howard had left a legacy of pre-planned torments to keep pushing Garrick over the edge. To Howard and his acolytes, it was nothing more than a sick psychological game. And as he neared the scene of his sister's murder, the stress-induced hallucinations returned.

Garrick slowly breathed in and blinked twice, erasing Emilie's face and restoring his own. He'd learned the hard way that panic prolonged the experience. When it had first happened at home in the bathroom, his reaction had terrified his girlfriend, Wendy, who has carried their child. Fearing stressing her out and added to his panic. As is often the case, a cool, calm head quickly resolved the problem.

He splashed the water across his face and dabbed it dry with a paper towel from the dispenser next to the tiny sink. He prayed that he'd find some salvation on this trip, or at least a modicum of closure on the torment that had been dogging him since Emilie's death. As a police detective, he regularly dealt with families picking up the pieces of a murdered loved one. It was a brutal side to life that most people didn't have to deal with. However, now he knew what *they* were going through, and that sense of pain and loss was beyond description. Closure was not an option. It was a necessity. He had to do this for himself, and for Wendy who'd driven him to the airport, kissed him softly and smiled as she made him promise not to do anything silly.

Then she'd pressed his palm gently against her stomach, over their child growing inside. He had every reason to move on.

All he had to do was take the step. What was stopping him?

2

PHILOSOPHERS HAD SUGGESTED that life was one giant cycle of cause and effect. Religious leaders pushed this notion and introduced concepts such as karma or heaven and hell. Scientists took the idea and forged laws and steadfast rules governed by impenetrable mathematics. But Philip E. Grant didn't have the patience for such esoteric ramblings. And he didn't have the time to think too deeply. For him, life was a binary state. It can be given. And it can be taken.

The claw hammer came down with such force it jolted from his hand and sent a shockwave of pain rippling up his left arm. The crunch of bone was satisfying, as was the spatter of warm blood that sprayed across his cheek. But it did little to quell the screams coming from the paralysed man bound across the table. Philip E. Grant shushed him, as one would a child, and like most parents he wished he were deaf so as not to hear the irritating whining. He should have gagged him, but that would have spoiled the aesthetic. And after months of planning, this had turned into a rush job.

Picking the hammer up, Philip felt the weight slipping it from his damp grip. He splayed his palm and wiped the blood from it across the twitching man's trouser leg. Philip brought the heavy metal head down again and again, jumping from his feet to transfer his body weight into each assault. A cracking jawbone changed the screams to a wet gargle as his victim drowned in his own blood. Soft brain matter reminded him a shoving his hand into a bag of candy as a tenacious youth and scooping the gelatinous contents out in one go. He'd squeeze them tightly together before rubbing them across his own arse crack and forcing his neighbour's little sister to eat them. She'd always cry. He'd always laugh. It was all good fun.

Lost in a daydream of halcyon times, Philip hadn't realised the noise had finally stopped. Blood flowed readily from the man's head, the top half of which resembled a cracked egg with a running yolk. Philip admired the artwork he had created. But he still had a way to go before it was perfect.

He briefly wondered why he had made life so difficult for himself before remembering this was his purpose. The final act. The denouement of a symphony he had been part of and was eager to play out until the end.

He took a break for coffee. He had a long night ahead, and the welcome package needed to be ready. Philip E. Grant may be many things, but impolite wasn't one of them.

3

_____

3

THE INTERIOR of the Ford Explorer was so cavernous that Garrick mused he could park his car inside with room to spare. In the short while he'd set foot in North America, it was very clear that there was no concept as *big enough*. At least from his parochial British point of view.

He and Molly were greeted by Kamila Ortega, a sassy Hispanic New Yorker who had hysterically waved her arms at the arrival gate while blowing kisses with each hand. A good deal shorter and heavier than Garrick, Kamila had crushed the breath from him in an uncomfortably long hug, while huskily reaffirming how delighted she was to finally meet him, while at the same time weighing him down with sombre condolences for losing his sister. Molly was barely able to slide a word in as she introduced Kamila as their US producer and fixer. Kamila a force marched them outside to a waiting car, where a lean, stubble-clad Scott Armstrong was waiting for them. Introduced as their driver cum cameraman, Scott was a soft-spoken thirty-something. He helped load their cases into the trunk, jamming the extra baggage next to a stack of silver-coloured flight cases packed with equipment for the shoot. He smiled but said a few words. Kamila slapped him on the back and pointed out he was from Iowa, as if that explained everything. Within minutes, they were heading down Interstate 57 on a four-hour trip to Flora.

Garrick sat at the back of the vehicle, slouched across the third row of cream leather seats, and enjoying the sumptuousness. It was better than business class. Molly sat in the middle row, her attention mostly on her phone as Kamila twisted around in the front passenger seat alternatively asking for details of their flight and outlining the schedule for the next few days.

Garrick tuned out the conversation and peered through the window, lost in thought. He'd read the schedule while back at home in Kent, and even then, it hadn't seemed quite real. He was used to the irregular rhythm of the police station. When a case was in, the pressure was relentless. There was never enough time, people, or mental capacity to worry about life outside work. Then there were the periods of admin which slothfully meandered between investigations. Then Molly Meyers had given him an opportunity to put his demons to rest.

Now he was in the car's backseat, using some of his rare holiday time to 'investigate' a deeply personal matter. He knew acutely that this was Molly's case to pursue and not his, and that it was a journalistic adventure, not a meaningful police matter. He wanted to gain closure from the experience but had no doubts that they would be no closer to answers than the official Flora Police Department or the FBI had reached.

A cramp in his index finger drew him back to the moment. He was clutching his iPhone far too tightly. It was switched on, but still in airplane mode because of the eye-watering mobile data costs his network had warned him about. He wanted to notify Wendy they'd landed safely, but she'd work that out for herself if there were no news reports of a crashed flight. He'd have to wait for a wi-fi connection before he could talk to her. It was just a little point, but it made him feel isolated. He was away from Wendy. Away from his team who had become a support network of sorts. He wondered if a case had come in that had DC's Fanta Liu and Harry Lord at loggerheads, with poor old Sean Wilkes stuck in the middle. If so, DS Chibarameze Okon was more than capable of dealing with it.

Pull yourself together, he thought to himself. He'd been in the States for less than two hours and he was already feeling pangs of homesickness. He had eight days to get through.

After less than an hour of monotonous freeway, Garrick struggled to stay awake as a wave of jetlag enveloped him. No matter how hard he tried to resist, it swamped him. The conversation between Molly and Kamila became an unclear murmur, and he regretted not sleeping on the plane. The car was too warm. The motion too soothing...

HE AWOKE FROM THE DEEPEST, warmest embrace he could recall. His head felt like it had been dipped in mist and he felt terribly disorientated. It was dark outside, and everything looked simultaneously familiar yet foreign.

"We're at the motel," Molly said as the electric side door slid open. "How did you sleep?"

Garrick tried to answer, but his mouth was dry, and he was feeling dehydrated. He followed Molly out. Kamila looped the long strap of her handbag, the leather delicately detailed in ancient Mayan images, and gave the motel a grand gesture.

"No expenses spent on our budget!" she declared with a snicker. "I'll check us in."

The eighties style EZ BREAK MOTEL neon sign hissed in the cool air, stretching between the three floors, built in a typical C-shaped footprint, with each of the room doors over-looking the parking lot. The paintwork was tired and flaking, and some of the windows covered in a layer of grime. It was more desperate than welcoming.

She briskly marched to the lit office at the corner of the complex with far too much energy for... what time? Garrick checked his watch, which he'd altered when they landed. It was only 7pm, but it felt as if days had passed.

"There is a diner just across the street if you're hungry." Molly pointed to a building with a flickering neon sign across the six wide lanes of traffic. It was too far for Garrick to make out the name. He shook his head.

"I just need to get my head down. I'll be fine in the morning."

"We will need to finish breakfast by about eight tomor-row. I'm guessing you're not used to jetlag." A playful smile flickered across her face as she suppressed a yawn. Garrick shook his head. "I bet you'll be awake about four in the morning, wide-eyed and raring to go."

"I doubt that very much."

Kamila returned with their keys, real metal ones on the end of a chunky plastic fob. Garrick was relieved to discover they were not sharing rooms. He needed his private space. He apologised to Scott who was single-handedly unloading the gear from the vehicle, took his suitcase and trundled it across to his room on the second floor. The lock was sticky, and it took two attempts before it opened. The room itself was basic, with a TV on the wall and linen on the hard bed. The bathroom was clean enough if you ignored the mould in the corners of the sink and shower and the strong stench of bleach. He twisted the security lock on the door, rolled his suitcase into the corner, and slumped on the bed, intending to have a shower.

He was asleep instantly.

As Molly Meyers had predicted, Garrick was wide awake at 4:36. Alerted by his rumbling stomach, he ignored it by logging onto the motel's free internet and messaging Wendy. He had several from her, all upbeat and expressing how much she already missed him. That was an exciting yet unusual feeling for him. She sent four lengthy messages back and waited with anticipation, hoping she'd reply, but nothing came. She was having later mornings in bed as the pregnancy progressed. Garrick had joked that she was trying to get as much sleep as possible before the birth. That reminded him he should really read up on the whole parenthood thing, as he didn't have a clue what was in store for them.

After longingly staring at the reply line for far too long, he had a shower and spent the rest of the morning hours blankly flicking through TV channels, marvelling how almost every commercial for medicine came with a list of side effects that included death. Why anybody would contemplate buying them was beyond him. He shook his head. What a country. His zombified cycling through the channels was mercifully halted when, at six o'clock, Molly knocked on the door and asked if he was joining them for breakfast.

Again, the diner offered the subtlest culture shock that fascinated him. The vast range of breakfast options on the menu was daunting. Back home he was used to three or four choices and that was it. When it came to ordering eggs, Scott, Kamila, and Molly were almost in tears at the perplexed expression etched across his face. When he stuttered the phrase, "I just want my eggs cooked *normally,*" the waitress shook her head and made the choice for him.

Breakfast conversation was light and darting between topics. Scott told him how he used to be a cameraman for a local Iowa news channel, which mostly involved filming county fairs, the aftermath of car chases, or the carnage from an occasional twister. Kamila never let slip any personal information – other than actively promoting her recent divorce. Through a series of name drops – none of which Garrick knew - she clearly saw herself as a major player in the documentary field. Garrick didn't buy into that, but kept silent. To him it was clear she was pinning a lot of her hopes on her liaison with Molly Meyers and the BBC, hopeful that it would send more business her way.

The actual reason they were all here was not mentioned at all. Molly was her usual self, the bubbly girl-from-Kent persona that Garrick had come to know. When she relaxed her Estuary accent crept back, a far cry from the serious image she portrayed on screen. The others may not have noticed, but he noticed she was hiding behind a personal wall hewn from her horrific experience at being kidnapped at the hands of the Murder Club. She kept her hand curled, resting the palm of the other over to it to conceal the missing finger that had been amputated by her captor. A malicious act that was nothing more than a taunt towards Garrick. It was the same digits that his sister had been forced to hack off when she fled her captors. The Murder Club certainly had a thing for symmetry and coincidences. Molly bravely wore the mental scars of her ordeal and used it to shape her own media career. It was opportunistic, not that Garrick could blame her.

There were a couple of moments between the laughter and idle chitchat, that he regretted the decision to come along. It would have been so much easier to stay at home, working on a case that would have absorbed all his attention and kept him away from exploring his own emotional baggage.

Molly paid the bill, leaving a generous tip that Garrick thought was another culturally unusual way of doing things. Why not just pay the waitress a decent wage? Then again, the service was beyond anything he'd experienced back home. It was quick and cheerful and served as a reminder that he should be more flexible in his opinions and not so set in his ways.

Only as he approached their Ford Explorer in the parking lot, did it sink into that the next stop was where his sister's nightmare had started. A chill wind seeped through the layers of his Barbour and goose bumps puckered his arms. A sudden rush of fatigue struck him courtesy of jetlag, making his legs feel leaden. Almost refusing to make the final steps to their vehicle.

He reminded himself why he was here. It wasn't for answers. It was for closure and the freedom to shape a new future with Wendy and his unborn child.

The worst was behind him.

4

4

FLECKS of white danced between fine raindrops as the breeze from the north intensified. It softened the harsh edges of the enormous barn standing at the entrance to the ranch. For Garrick, it was a familiar sight he'd seen on photographs of the murder scene sent by the Flora PD. The large double hangar doors led into a grain silo. The metal doors themselves had tarnished to an autumnal brown, but retained a sense of impenetrability. It was here that his sister had been trapped as her pursuers closed the heavy door on her hand, forcing her into the impossible choice of being caught – or sawing off her own fingers to free herself.

Several miles northeast of the small town of Flora, this had been the location Emilie and her fiancé, Sam McKinzie, had sought refuge during a snowstorm. The details were muddied, and without witnesses the full story would never emerge. Only fragmented evidence painted the picture, and Garrick was all too aware that evidence and cold hard facts were two very different things.

His sister's rental car was found at the back of the property. It was nothing more than a burned-out husk, but the dented fender indicated they may have been in some sort of minor collision, although that could have occurred at any point on their road trip. Sam was found inside the property, his chest cavity hacked apart while he was still alive. Whether or not Emilie witnessed this, Garrick would never know.

Images of mutilated bodies flashed in his mind's eye as he stared at the building. The Sergeant dealing with the case, Al Howard, had sent him some selected images when he'd learned that Garrick was a police detective. They showed several victims spread across the site, all murdered over a few days, as if part of some initiation rite.

Emilie wasn't amongst them. Other than her fingers, there was no other indication where her body lay. Months later, saliva and blood samples were found in an abandoned car across the state line, mixed with that of a Korean woman who had also gone missing and was now presumed dead.

Perhaps Emilie had been hiding in the killer's car when she was discovered. If the FBI had obtained any further information about that, then they were keeping it as privileged information. Until that point, Garrick had kept an open line of communication with Sergeant Howard, although he wasn't very forthcoming with details and Garrick became increasingly frustrated with their lack of progress. And when the FBI took over, that seam of information dried up. The only new information he had come from

Molly Meyer's persistent investigation into what had happened.

Garrick shivered in the cold. The rain increased, and he dug his hands deeper into his coat pockets but made no motion to raise his hood. The cold rain on his face made him feel alert. He slowly arced around the building, taking in the building's length and the circular grain silo at the far end. This was the killing floor. No matter how many images he had seen of the ranch, they didn't do the scale of it any justice.

A hundred yards further back there was a single-story ranch house, complete with ubiquitous porch and a water tower behind. Garrick had scrutinised the ranch using Google Earth, hoping to find something the officers on the ground had overlooked. A pointless exercise, but one that prevented him from feeling completely redundant.

The landowner had been one of the victims found at the scene. The property had since passed to his children who lived in Florida and were desperate to sell it, but as it was still part of an FBI investigation, they couldn't. Molly couldn't find any connection between the owner and John Howard, the inaugural member of the Murder Club who had befriended Garrick back in the UK and seemed hellbent on torturing him, even from beyond the grave. John Howard had been here when Emilie and Sam had been murdered. He had somehow lured her to commit the deed. The working assumption was that Howard and his accomplices had attacked the owner in preparation for their orgy of violence.

He felt a gentle squeeze on his elbow. Molly Meyers had sidled up to him, wielding a large black umbrella to keep her dry and camera-ready. She had exchanged her Nike trainers for black knee-high boots, which were already flecked with mud. Her liquid green eyes studied him carefully.

"How're you feeling?"

Garrick struggled to find the words, and ended up with an unconvincing, "okay."

Despite reluctance from the local police, Molly had secured access to the ranch for filming, but they only had half a day to do so. Scott and Kamila were already unpacking equipment from the car.

"We're going to get some coverage of the ranch from the outside. And some shots of me walking around looking thoughtful," she managed a wry smile. "If you want to go in alone..." she gestured towards the hangar.

Garrick nodded. The last thing he wanted was to be emotional around the others. That wasn't the British way. On the drive to the ranch, the atmosphere in the car had gone from good-natured to walking on eggshells.

Molly gave him a gentle pat on the back, then turned to join the others. Garrick sucked in a long breath and walked towards the imposing doors. Each step felt heavy, and his stomach gnawed with the weight of an enormous fat-based breakfast. He could feel his heart hammering in his chest. He wondered if this was the onset of a panic attack. It was an unfamiliar feeling. Despite his recent mental health issues, David Garrick had always been a confident and self-assured person. At least he thought so. Years of flat-footing the streets as a regular police constable, before becoming a detective had hardened him to the vilest avenues of human behaviour and nothing fazed him when it came to the dark depths of human psyche.

However, *this* was personal.

He thought he had the willpower to confront his demons,

but with each step his doubts clawed at him. Raking from the scar on his head, across his heart, and slowly pulled him into the earth.

He struggled to a walk forwards along on the dust road, which was now more of a layer of mud and gravel as the weather deteriorated. Each step was heavier than the last. Reaching the doors, he ran a hand over the rusted surface. A heavy vertical lever at chest height was the only visible means of opening them. With trembling hands, Garrick gripped the shaft and pulled to the right and down. The aging mechanism squeaked in protest and a dull clunk reverberated across the surface as the two halves parted slightly. He lent his weight to drag one open. It grumbled across a rail as it begrudgingly slid open. Even with his body mass behind it, it took all his effort to move it. A flow of stale air issued out like a dying wheeze. The doors could probably take a bomb blast, and Garrick was reminded that the previous owner was a prepper, convinced the world was about to end and he could ride the storm on his ranch. He'd probably invested heavily in battling a nuclear winter, a biohazard attack, hordes of marauding Mad Max-type bikers – but he'd come unstuck with a middle-aged British psychopath knocking at his door one fateful day.

The room beyond was dark, lit only by the shaft of light from the opening door. It was a large concrete space marred by oil stains. Garrick had seen the pictures of multiple vehicles stored here. A large RV, several jeeps, and a motorbike that had belonged to the owner but had since been impounded. A door opposite was the only way onwards. The peeling red paint and push bar to unlock it reminded him of a fire escape. He imagined Emilie running for her life, threading her way through the parked vehicles, trying each door in turn in the hope one of them was unlocked, before making a dash for the hangar doors.

He imagined her opening them a crack to slip through, before her pursuers tried to crush her, trapping her fingers. Taunting her with a painful death that would welcome her as they wrestled to open the door to seize her.

His footsteps echoed from the vaulted ceiling as he kept to the bridge of light seeping directly to the far door. What had led John Howard to select this remote ranch? What connections were being made in his mind to lure Emilie and Sam here? What did he hope to achieve by creating his sadistic network in the first place?

The official line was that John Howard was an ex-Falklands conflict veteran, suffering from PTSD. But his sadistic tendencies existed before then. The war was just a convenient canvas for him to commit atrocities and meet like-minded people. That was the part Garrick couldn't get his head around. John Howard was an intellectual who had intentionally befriended him. It was a false friendship, merely a rouse for John Howard to study him as a scientist looked down on a rat. The man found pleasure in killing as if it were a sport amongst his fellow murderers. Was it a cult? It felt like one, governed by a sick mind who manipulated others to do his deeds. Even after his death, those affiliates continued the plan against him – or as Garrick was starting to think of it, an experiment – to its ultimate conclusion.

That had been thwarted, thanks to his diligent team, and the surprising help of MET detective Oliver Kane who had been investigating Garrick, suspecting him of being one of John Howard's clique. The MET police force was conducting further investigations to see just how far the decay had seeped, from the police commissioner, upwards into whoever at Whitehall had turned a blind eye to Howard's military rampage.

Now David Garrick was here he understood there would be no resolution. No magic answers. The FBI investigation had gone on for so long it stank of rapidly becoming a cold case: it had a hint of conspiracy. *The beast was dead. Let's not look too deeply into reasons or motivations in case we don't like what we find.*

Garrick reached the door and snorted at the notion of a conspiracy. He knew madness lay that way. He pushed the bar on the door, and it swung silently open on well-tended hinges despite the year that had passed since it was last used. He stood on the threshold of the darkness beyond. It was impenetrable. He fished his mobile phone from his pocket and thumbed the flashlight, noticing that he hadn't charged his battery since the plane, and it was already half-drained. He cast the weak beam across the new room.

It was an empty cavernous space. The weak illumination gave hints of machinery leading into the curved far wall where the hangar met the grain silo and disappeared into the deeper shadows of a large hatch. Chains stretched from the rafters far above, tipped with industrial cargo hooks. Garrick could imagine what use the corrupt minds would have put them to. Imagines of the blood-spattered tables that once stood in the room came unbidden to him. This was the killing floor where John Howard and his cohorts imagined they were turning death into art. The bastard had even sold lamps with shades made from human skin, bespoke collectibles for sick-minded collectors.

He stepped into the hall and shivered. It was ice cool here, as if the souls of the dead still haunted the place...

He shook that notion from his mind. He was a practical

man, with no space in his world view for the supernatural. He even struggled with religion. He had seen visions of his sister. Heard bodiless voices, but all were the work of the tumour pressing against his brain, that had now hopefully been vanquished forever.

It was here Sam McKenzie – his brother-in-law to be – was brutally murdered. The coroner's report made bleak reading. His assailants had stripped away the flesh from his face and neck while he was still alive. He could imagine the laughter and jeering from the assembled mob. How many would there be? Three, four... or more?

Police forensics indicated there had been nine different cars on site but couldn't say over what period. Maybe all at once. Perhaps one at a time. None had been traced. The killers themselves showed a deep understanding of forensics and, despite the carnage they'd wrought, they hadn't left behind a modicum of evidence.

Garrick stood in the centre of the room. Lifting his phone aloft, he could just see the gantry above where the chains rolled freely on rails. A conveyor belt ran along the back wall, through into the silo. The silence was so absolute he could hear the blood pounding in his ears. There was no patter of rain on the roof. No hint that Molly was filming outside. He gauged the walls were reinforced. It was prepper heaven.

Had had braced himself for a tsunami of emotions, but all he felt was detachment. Sam had died here, as had others. Presumably killed in front of Emilie. Somehow, she had broken free and made a run for her life.

There was nothing left to see. No more evidence left to extract. This place was nothing more than a slice of macabre history that had left an indelible stain on those linked to the victims, but otherwise it will have passed unnoticed by the rest of the world. Exactly like every other crime scene back home. They were places of cruelty. Passion. Vengeance. But ultimately, those moments were lost in time. Consigned to memory.

Garrick felt an overwhelming urge to leave. Not just this place, but the country. There was nothing for him here.

5

DAVID GARRICK SUSPECTED that Molly was a little disappoint
with his reaction. Although she'd promised he wouldn't
appear on camera, he couldn't shake the thought that she
wanted to interview him at the scene of the crime, or at least
get some footage of the brooding brother casting his eye over
the ranch.

Instead, he sat in the Explorer as the rain increased and
the crew followed Molly into the hangar. Scott ran back and
forth as he set up three portable redhead lights, powered by a
small diesel genny stashed in the boot. It took at least an hour
before they started filming inside.

Rain gently pattered on the windows, and the flecks of
snow increased. Garrick toyed with his phone on the off
chance there was a wi-fi network around. There was nothing.

Not even a phone signal. He wondered what Wendy was doing back home. It was almost lunchtime for him, so she would perhaps be visiting her parents for dinner, or hanging out with Sonia, her friend from the hiking group who had a knack of rubbing Garrick up the wrong way. At least now he was pleased that Wendy had company.

Finally, the side door slid open, waking Garrick from the nap he'd fallen into. Molly ducked inside, shaking the rain from her jacket.

"That's a wrap here." She frowned at him. "Do you want to take another look around?"

Garrick shook his head. "I'm done. There's nothing here for me."

She sat down in the middle row, leaning on the seat to look at him. "Not even questions?"

"There are always questions."

"Well, a few more occurred to me now we're here, walking in her footsteps." She waited for his response, but Garrick was poker faced. "How did Emilie escape? Or rather, how come she managed it, but three men who were also killed here couldn't?"

"Luck."

"And she was trapped by the door. The way I see it, she was trying to close it behind her."

"To trap her attackers inside."

Molly nodded. "But you've moved that door. It's heavy. That seems like far too much effort to stall somebody. And a man," she gestured towards him, "would presumably have more strength than somebody like me. So they could've opened it quickly."

"When you're running for your life. When fear grips you, rational thinking is the first casualty." Garrick had seen the effects of that countless times. Some unfortunate victims had the perfect chance to escape snatched away from them because of their own dumb mistakes.

Molly nodded thoughtfully. The tailgate opened, admitting a blast of cool air as Scott and Kamila began ferrying flight cases of equipment from the building. Garrick felt guilty for not offering to help, but he was too tired to even offer.

"I wonder why she had the saw," Molly said as the tailgate closed. She caught Garrick's look. "She sawed her own fingers off." She held up her hand to show her severed digit. "The terror she must have felt to do that... I can only imagine. But she did it with a hacksaw."

"The coroner said some victims were sawed up. I imagine she got the saw and maybe used it to free herself. It could've been the only weapon she had access to." Molly nodded again, but her brow furrowed. Garrick sighed and held up his hand. "Okay, Molly, what's really on your mind?"

Her eyes strayed to the hangar, watching Scott struggle to carry the flight case with the lighting gear inside. Garrick followed her gaze.

"This all circles back to John Howard. He lured her here, somehow. He knew of her travel plans. He wanted her here. He wanted her to get to you."

As he listened, Garrick's focus shifted from the cameraman to the raindrops meandering down the glass. He watched as some merged and increased in speed, colliding again and again to reach their destination at the bottom of the window. A random series of intersection that led to an inevitable single conclusion.

Molly continued. "Everything was premeditated to the nth degree."

"What's your point?"

"Did that include her escape? I mean, Emilie, above anybody else. She cut off her fingers and left them behind... evidence they could have easily destroyed but left in place. It all feels targeted specifically at you."

Garrick gave a humourless chuckle. "Seems I am the centre of the universe, after all."

Molly opened her mouth to say something more, but thought better of it as the tailgate opened again. An idea was still nagging her, but she forced a smile.

"Well, it's lunch if you can stomach it. Then this afternoon we're interviewing Sergeant Howard who was running the case."

Garrick raised his eyebrows in appreciation. He was looking forward to finally meeting the only man he knew who had a connection to the investigation. The irony of the name wasn't lost on him. It was one of those things. A coincidence.

"This is a bad time." Sergeant Al Howard held up his hand to usher Molly aside, but she refused to move and blocked his path as he tried to exit Flora's police station and cross towards his cruiser.

"We had an appointment booked in for a couple of weeks," Molly said firmly. "You were one of the first people I called when I knew this was on."

The Sergeant's sinewy, lean build tensed, and his jaw muscles worked hard as he ground his teeth. Even talking civilly, his harsh Chicago accent was embedded into Garrick's mind as that of a stereotypical movie mobster. He sucked in a sharp breath, placing both hands on his hips as he raised himself to his full six-foot two height.

"I'm sorry about that, ma'am," he said with deliberate patience. "But there's been a murder. I apologise if the killer hadn't scheduled that with you."

He pushed past her and continued towards his black Ford 4x4 with the word POLICE slashed along the side. Garrick couldn't help but smile. Even their vehicles were cooler than the ones back home.

Molly threw a desperate look in Garrick's direction, then raised her arms to the heavens as she shouted after the Sergeant.

"Then let us come with you. Get some footage of the brave sergeant in action. It will make excellent b-roll." Howard stopped, the driver's door half open. Seeing that she'd hooked him, Molly pressed on. "You can have a say on what we can use. Your case. It will make a cool 'hero shot' for the entire piece."

The officer's shoulder tensed, then his head sagged, and he peered over his shoulder. "Okay. You do what I say." He rapped the roof of the vehicle. "Keep up."

He hadn't even climbed in his car and closed the door when Molly was racing back to their own vehicle, madly waving her arms.

"Let's go! Let's go!"

Within moments, Scott gunned the engine and their tyres shrieked on the wet asphalt as he rushed to keep up with the cop who was speeding ahead with red warning lights blazing and the siren whooping. Garrick felt a rush of adrenaline wash away the jet lag. He'd had more than his fair share his share of chases recently, but the basic buzz that came from good old-fashioned police call out was like catnip to him.

The traffic ahead on both sides of the road parted like the Red Sea as they passed, barely slowing down at intersections and jumping every red light. Scott crushed his body closer to the wheel as he gripped it tightly. Kamila leaned over her seat and struggled to pull the camera out of its case. Molly was swaying back and forth in her seat, comb in one hand and mirror in the other as she attempted to look 'camera ready.' She wanted Scott and Kamila ready to roll as soon as they stopped, so was issuing a torrent of instructions about what they should film. Garrick wisely stayed quietly in the back.

They tore through the heart of Flora, which looked exactly as Garrick imagine it would. Convenience stores and familiar junk food restaurants peppered between diners and unfamiliar chain stores. Then they were skimming on the outskirts of an industrial estate. Ahead, through the rain-soaked windshield they could see a wall of red emergency lights. Three police cruisers had parked horizontally across the parking lot to limit access. A pair of ambulances stood closer to a warehouse, with a fire truck alongside. Their crews milled outside, seemingly reluctant to go in.

Scott almost tail-ended Sergeant Howard as he skidded to a halt. He snatched the camera from Kamila and jumped out of the car, leaving the door open. Kamila kept back as Molly and Garrick hurried out.

Howard pulled a *police* emblazoned poncho over his head as he approached the cops hanging outside an open warehouse door.

"What've we got?"

"A complete mess, Sarge." The middle-aged uniformed woman indicated the camera. Howard made a dismissive motion.

"Ignore 'em. They're with me."

The cop shrugged, clearly not enamoured with having a TV crew get under their feet. She led Howard into the warehouse. The rain sounded like hailstones on the transparent roof panels that provided the bulk of illumination. Eight wooden shipping crates had been moved to the centre of the space and draped in a large green canvas drape. It formed a twelve-foot-tall pyramid plinth, with each fold artfully arcing up to a large glass tank. Light from above refracted in the liquid that filled it to the brim. It was a perfect cube and suspended inside was a body.

Garrick felt his stomach knot. He didn't need to look around to get a measure of the people in the room. Out of the corner of his eye, he saw Scott hesitate. The camera mounted on his shoulder bobbed towards the ground before he raised it again to focus on the macabre image. Sergeant Howard put one hand on his hips, the other rubbing across his mouth as he sharply inhaled. Molly stood close to his right, and he caught her sharp intake of breath.

"The hell is this?" Howard muttered. He slowly walked forward, circling around the crime scene. Scott followed, keeping his distance so he could keep the cop in the same frame as the victim.

Even from afar, Garrick could see the scars across the corpse's face. An inch-wide scars of badly sewn puckered flesh ran from the bridge of the nose to the jaw muscles. It distorted the face, but he was pretty sure it was a man whose black hair was pulled tightly back. The skull had been smashed, shaped into some sort of angular Frankenstein parody. His face was angled down, the right arm outstretched to the top corner of the tank, the other to the bottom corner. Clad in blue medical scrubs, he was resting on his knees, as if bowing. The killer had intentionally set out to create a macabre art installation. The logistics of the entire setup were staggering, and Garrick instinctively knew it wasn't the work of a single killer - which raised disturbing connections to the defunct Murder Club.

And he couldn't shake the feeling that this was targeted at him, but he knew better than suggest that to Howard. Swapping a brief look with Molly confirmed she was thinking the same. It couldn't be a coincidence.

Sergeant Howard completed a lap of the crates, joining the policewoman who hadn't taken her eyes off the sculpture.

"Have you ever seen anything like this?" she muttered.

Howard shook his head. "Only in the movies. Notify CSI what they're in for."

Garrick finally found his motor skills and stepped forward for a closer look. He scanned the floor, noticing it was impeccably clean for a warehouse. He looked between the warehouse door and the emergency fire escape at the rear. They looked intact, a hint that the killer had full access to the building, which meant they would have had all the time needed to set up the scene. The scene was far too contrived to be a random artistic impulse. He sensed there was meaning to the display, but all he could think about was the sense of theatre deliberately conjured.

Halfway around, he could tell the liquid in the tank was thick enough to keep the corpse poised. Garrick paused when he became aware that Sergeant Howard was glaring at him.

"It seems this stuff follows you around." They were the first words he'd spoken directly to Garrick.

Garrick pulled himself together and approached Howard with his hand outstretched. "David Garrick."

"I know." Howard made no motion to shake the offered

hand, and Garrick was damned if he was going to lower it. "I've followed your career, especially when Ms Meyers," he bobbed his head in Molly's direction, "coerced me into talking to you both." With great reluctance, he gripped Garrick's hand in a vice-like grip and gave it a single shake. "From what I've been told, this kinda thing is normal over the pond."

"Not exactly." Garrick was about to continue, but Howard headed him off.

"But not here. And let me remind you, here you're a civilian."

It was a pointed drawing of the line. Howard angled his head to do his best to peer down at Garrick.

"Of course, Sergeant. I'm not interested in a pissing match. Even if it's exactly this sort of thing that happens around here more than once." He flashed a friendly smile, but he had no intention of being the meek Brit or listening to trite *'that's not how we do things here'* lines that he expected Howard to say. He caught Molly tense at the stand-off. She didn't see the flicker of Howard's eyebrow. A stoic sign of respect.

Howard turned his attention back to the body. "What's your take?"

"I suppose the logical thing would be a copycat." Garrick examined the corpse's face. The eyelids had been removed. "But people who do this sort of thing don't follow logic. This tells me they're still out there. They were waiting for this moment."

6

6

THEY HAD STAYED at the warehouse until the CSI team arrived and ushered them away. To Molly's surprise, Sergeant Howard hadn't interfered with what they filmed. She had tried to get a sound bite with him, but he muttered that now wasn't the time.

Regrouping in a dinner, Scott took great glee in reviewing his footage, which Kamila refused to watch.

"I don't enjoy looking at that kinda thing," she said, shooing the camera away.

Molly filled her iPad with notes, typing with one hand while ravenously shovelling food into her mouth with the other. Garrick was grateful that nobody was asking him his thoughts.

He logged into the diner's complimentary wi-fi and

checked his emails. There was one from Wendy. It was nothing more than a summary of visiting her parents the previous night and a plan to have lunch with Sonia today. Looking at the time on his phone, he made a quick calculation and assumed she was now asleep. They should really schedule a phone call. He missed her voice and desperately wanted to talk about what had just happened. The emphasis was on talking, not listening to Molly or anybody else's opinion. He understood there was the chance that it was a coincidence. That he was in the wrong place at the wrong time. That the Murder Club was in the rear-view mirror, being tied up back home. But...

He finished reading the email, which neatly summarised that she was feeling well and craving blueberries. A quick miss you ended the message. Garrick glanced at the time again and quickly wrote:

MISSING YOU MORE! *Started filming today. It's all a little weird being here, but I'm fine.*

HIS FINGERS HOVERED over the keyboard as he considered elaborating. He knew it was too short, so added:

JET LAG IS TERRIBLE. *Speak soon xx*

HE HESITATED AGAIN - THEN QUICKLY HIT SEND before he could undo the anaemically worded email. Conversation filtered across the table, mostly from Kamila about how they need to stay on schedule and not allow new developments to derail them. Already, Howard had blocked any chance of a further interview for the rest of the day, which meant they had to reschedule it for tomorrow morning - which in turn prevented them from driving to the State border where the car containing Emile's DNA was discovered. Kamila had set up an interview with the patrol officer who had discovered the automobile, so that would be bumped to the following day too. She was more irritated that a random murder had disrupted their schedule on day one.

A hasty rearrangement was made, which would mean capturing establishing footage of Flora and Molly talking to camera around the town, talking about the investigation, and even recording the conclusion, all of which would be edited into the correct sequence.

Half a day into the trip, and Garrick was growing aware that he was an increasingly redundant component. He wasn't needed for the shoot. Visiting the ranch of horrors had done nothing to dampen his emotions. Poor Sam and others had been slaughtered there, which was terrible, but he still felt detached from events. The cold fact was that Emilie hadn't been killed there. That had happened elsewhere. Her body was still un-recovered. Maybe it would be found one day, but he knew the odds were against it after all this time.

Time...

The timing of this new incident was peculiar. He had only just arrived, and such a venture would have required weeks of planning. Which, if it was aimed at him, meant knowledge of his plans back in the UK. Even he had been unsure what he was doing until almost the last week when Molly had confirmed the trip. She had Kamila, Scott, and others over here, preparing for the shoot. So did that mean...?

He shook that thought away. He was now delving into the world of paranoia. Garrick was a pragmatist. The world was only out to get you if you believed it was. Perhaps it was jet lack, but he felt himself suddenly sinking into his seat as fatigue melted through him. He needed to go back to the motel and sleep. Molly gave him a curious look when he announced his intentions, but said nothing. Perhaps she was disappointed in his muted reaction at being here after all the effort and cost she had put into the trip. Scott offered to drop him off, while the others stayed in the diner to plan what they were going to record. Dark grey clouds mustered, and the rain transformed into snow, which melted on contact with the ground. The cameraman talked little during the short drive, while Garrick fought to keep his eyes open. By the time Garrick closed and locked his motel door, it was all he could manage to kick off his shoes and toss his coat across the only seat in the corner of the room. He was asleep on the bed almost instantly.

A POUNDING on the door woke him up. Confusion swirled as Garrick took in the unfamiliar room. It took several seconds of foggy recall to recap events. He sat on the edge of the bed, still full clothed, as the pounding on the door occurred again. Blurry-eyed, his hand padded the crumped bed sheet for his phone. He eventually found it in his pocket. The screen remained dark when he tapped it. Presumably the battery had died.

He crossed to the door and peered through the spyhole. Sergeant Howard was standing outside. Garrick quickly opened the door as Howard was about to knock again.

"Sergeant?"

"Garrick. I figured you were comatose in there."

"The jet lag is knocking me sideways. What's happened?"

"You weren't answering your phone, and I thought you might wanna be at the coroner's office to see what we find."

Garrick blinked in surprise at the generous offer. "An autopsy? You guys move fast."

"CSI don't enjoy waiting around."

"Sure. That would be useful. Is Molly there already?"

The corner of Howard's mouth twitched. "Ms Meyer isn't invited. This is just a courtesy from one professional to another. It's not a reality show."

Garrick nodded in understanding. He took his coat from the chair and made sure he had the room key, before stepping out into the chilly night. Snow was falling heavier now, and the temperature had plummeted enough to make him shiver. Only when he sat in the passenger seat of the police 4x4 did he notice the time: 21:13. He'd slept right through the afternoon.

Howard didn't make small talk as he drove across town to the coroner's office. Garrick cranked the side window down an inch, so the cold air blasting inside woke him up. He took in the subtle difference between the American and British police vehicles. The cluster of a GPS screen and chunky police radio were more familiar. The 12-gauge shotgun holstered in a metal frame near his leg in the passenger footwell was not. Although Garrick was familiar with firearms, Howard's Glock Model 21 holstered on his belt made him feel uneasy.

The radio crackled to life a few times with reports of minor incidents. Some kids hanging around a closed hardware stall. An automobile crammed with teenagers was reported jumping red lights to the east. It was rather mundane, not the endless violence Garrick had been expecting. They passed a bar with a flickering old neon sign that blacked out several letters but still lured in a handful of people hunched against the increasing wind and snow. The coroner's office was a single-floored building on the corner of the street a block away from a Mach 1 gas station.

Garrick pulled the collar of his Barbour tighter as he exited the vehicle, and the sharp wind stung his face.

"We're in for a helluva weather front," Howard growled without showing the slightest reaction to the plummeting temperatures. He led the way to the side door entrance and thumbed the intercom. Moments later, they were buzzed inside.

The grey corridor was poorly lit, and the heating was on full blast. The middle-aged woman sitting behind a reception desk smiled as she rearranged her glasses.

"Evening, Al."

Howard signed the visitor book. "Hi Maureen. How's Cleveland?"

With a distracted sigh, Maureen pulled a face as she typed with one finger on her ageing computer. "Still got his thyroid. He's now refusing to leave Clay City other than to go fishin'."

"You two shoulda got married, Mau."

"Livin' together is bad enough. Speakin' of which, the back door to this place is still faulty. Kids'll get in here if you're not careful."

Howard passed the pen to Garrick who added his name under the Sergeant's with only the merest acknowledgement from Maureen. A little more small talk was exchanged even as Howard strode down the corridor. Reaching the second shining steel-clad door on the left, he entered without knocking.

Doctor Dugu was a cheery, short, dumpy Korean man who nodded at both men the moment they entered. He was pulling on a white smock as he circled a central table. Sergeant Howard had no time to make introductions before the coroner was indicating a cadaver covered on a plastic sheet, laid out on the table in the centre of the room. The temperature was much cooler here, yet Garrick was sweating.

"Forensics had a dinky of a time getting him out of the tank. It was completely sealed with silicon."

"A custom job like that shouldn't be hard to track down," Garrick said.

Dugu shrugged as he rolled on a pair of blue Nitrile gloves. "I know they were disappointed there were no prints on the thing. Our John Doe here was suspended in a kinda gelatine. They're analysing it now."

"Like a pork pie?" Garrick caught the puzzled look from both men. "You don't have them here?"

Dugu carefully rolled the sheet from the naked body, releasing a pungent aroma of formaldehyde trapped beneath. Howard coughed as it caught his throat.

Doctor Dugu nodded. "Yup. There was a healthy dose of preservative in the liquid, which makes me think the murder was premeditated for a long time, not just cobbled together last minute. The skull has been smashed, and several limbs, too." He took a metal pointed from a tray of implements and indicated the scars running from the corner of the victim's eyes to the cheek muscles. "The wounds here were done with a sharp blade, possibly a scalpel. From the puckering of the flesh, I think it happened while the man was still alive."

"Conscious?" Howard asked, frowning as he leaned in.

"I would think so, but it's a straight, clean incision, so I'm guessing he was anesthetised at least. Even restrained, it's too clean a cut. Same with the eyelids. Both sliced off with care, although the blade scored the surface of the left eye."

"Making sure he could see everything..." Garrick muttered. "The poor sod couldn't look away."

The coroner nodded and traced the pointer down the scar to the cheek bone. "This here seems to be the reason for the incision. The muscles have been pulled with wire. Held in place to keep the victim smiling."

Garrick and Howard exchanged a puzzled glance. Neither man had noticed the expression when they'd found the victim, and the deeper meaning behind the awful torture was not immediately apparent.

Dugu continued. "There are neater ways to achieve that, but that was the outcome." He shuffled to the side of the table and used the pointer to circle around the fingers. "Wiring was used here too, to hold had the fingers and make sure the indexes of both hands were pointing." The hands still kept the shape, with a coil of wire snaking around the digits to hold them in place. "I'll remove the wires to see if they can get a partial print from them."

Garrick doubted the killer would be so clumsy to leave any such signs behind.

"What was the cause of death?" said Howard. Garrick noticed he'd stepped back several more paces than was necessary. He wondered if it was the sickly pickle smell from the body, or the Sergeant was putting on a brave face around the dead.

"I couldn't see any puncture wounds to suggest lethal injection. Head injury, perhaps." Dugu tapped the pointer thoughtfully on the edge of the table, the metallic clicking echoing through the room. "I'm gonna bet on drowning, but I'll have to remove the lungs to verify."

"Drowning in the gelatine?" asked Garrick.

Dugu nodded. "With his jaw wired open like that, I'd say so."

"But he'd been thrashing around surely?" said Howard.

"Not if he was completely paralysed," Garrick pointed out.

The coroner indicated the fingernails of one hand. "All his nails are clean. Either he was a very fastidious man, or the killer removed anything we could use to pinpoint where we as abducted or murdered."

"Which shows a deep level of understanding what we'd be looking for," muttered Garrick.

He noticed Howard react to the 'we,' but the officer let the comment slide.

"But..." Dugu moved to the feet and ran the pointer down the sole of one foot. "There is dirt in the whorls of the toes. Possibly from when he was stripped." He replaced the pointer on the tray and selected a scalpel. "Anyways, I'll open him up and run a full toxicology on him."

Howard circled the table, studying the entire body.

"It's a helluva lot of work to make a statement."

"But a statement to whom?" said Dugu. He didn't catch the glance Howard threw in Garrick's direction.

The door opened, and Maureen entered, holding a print-out. She didn't seem bothered by the corpse on the table or the pungent smell hanging in the room.

"We have an email about your lad, here," she gestured to the corpse. "He's been identified." She handed the note to Garrick. He took it before she realised her mistake. "That ain't for you." She snatched the report back and handed it to Sergeant Howard.

The cop took his time reading it, slowly digesting the information before he wordlessly handed the printout to Garrick. Garrick felt the sergeant's full gaze boring into him as he read the email. The man was from Illinois and had been missing for a week. Garrick was drawn to the name. The familiar arrangement of letters that sent a chill through him. His legs became weak, threatening to collapse him to the floor as he re-read the victim's name.

It was a message, alright. A pointed one.

The name of the dead name on the table was *David Garrick.*

7

"YOU UNDERSTAND the complication this puts on my investigation?" The wooden chair creaked as Segreant Howard sat back, his arms folded. He peered at Garrick from beneath his eyebrows.

Garrick's hand was shaking as he sipped the Jack Daniels and Coke he'd ordered the moment they'd marched into the bar. The bartender had silently handed it over with a familiar nod in Howard's direction, then both men headed for a quiet corner. A group of locals played pool, winding down after work with easy laughter as they ribbed one another while glancing at the news playing on the televisions dotted around the car. To Garrick, the background noise was nothing more than a discordant hum. Something he struggled to identify as

English. For all he was concerned, they could've been anywhere in the world.

"I mean, I'm not sure whether to treat you as a victim or..."

Howard left the sentence unfinished.

"Or accomplice?" Garrick sipped the drink and sniggered. It burned his throat but tasted good. He wasn't really a drinker, and the last time he'd had any alcohol was just before Wendy had found out she was pregnant, and they'd knocked back several bottles of wine when Sonia had visited and stayed far too long.

He should tell Wendy. He pulled out his phone. The black screen reminded him he hadn't charged it and now the battery was dead. Just as well, he thought, as he reconsidered the impulse to talk to her. This is to sort of news that would frighten her. If the Club was still active, then she could be at risk. He'd assumed the Club had been destroyed, and their ranks came for all walks of society, so who could he trust to watch over her?

Fanta Liu, his young Detective Constable back in Kent, had the sense to keep things low key and was resourceful enough to know when to bypass official channels.

Or should it be Sonia? She saw Wendy almost every day, but Garrick didn't really know how reliable she was. His next thought was to contact DCI Oliver Kane. The men may not exactly be friends, but he was confident the London Detective would have his back. Plus, once Segreant Howard had filed his report, Garrick was certain the information would filter through to him. Howard broke his reverie.

"That's not what I meant."

Garrick swirled the half remaining measure of his drink. "If our roles are reversed, I'd say it. Of course, the prep involved in something like this..." he gesticulated to the window, to the unfriendly world outside.

"It means somebody over here was talking to somebody on your side. We better start getting some lines of enquiry going."

Garrick stared into space. When it was apparent he would not speak, Howard continued.

"Let's start with the obvious. Your Ms Meyers."

Garrick knocked back another mouthful of drink. Each one was becoming tastier, while making his head foggier. Perfect to forget the nightmare unfolding around him.

"Do you know all about Molly's ordeal at the hands of these killers?"

"I've read the reports. What's your take?"

"She's suffered mental persecution, physical terror. Even mutilation. The fact she is even here is a testimony to her courage."

"Or a testimony to her ambition." He clocked Garrick's troubled frown. "I'm looking at this all objectively. A reporter goes from a local hack to a major news channel, covering international stories. All because of you. Focused on you. Why? Because you were some bigshot Sherlock Holmes figure? Why latch on to some no-name detective? No offence," he added after a longer than comfortable pause.

Garrick necked back the rest of the drink. "You know Sherlock Holmes wasn't a real person, right?"

Judging from the cascade of micro-expressions flitting across the sergeant's face, he wasn't too sure. The truth was the remarks cut to Garrick's nerves more than he liked to admit. Not that he could believe that for a second, but the assault on him directly had been so surgical, so precise, it *felt* plausible. And that was the problem with John Howard's entire scheme. Even the most bizarre elements basked in the reflections of reality. They manipulated his own perceptions of himself. Toyed with his fragile mental health as his illness progressed. It made him even doubt almost every aspect of his life. And now it seemed as if his punishment wasn't over.

He firmly put the glass down with a solid thump. "I trust Molly Meyers. She's one of the few people I can say that about. If it's the same people behind this, then spending any time focusing on her is exactly what they want you to do." He stabbed a finger towards the outside world. "The minds behind this are masters of illusion and deception. They want you to look over here," he waved a hand, "while the trick happens over here." He twiddled the fingers of his other hand.

Howard gave a mirthless smile. "Which is why magicians have a glamourous assistant to look at. Y'know who actually does the illusion? It's the woman in the box. The magician is the one waving his arms as a distraction."

Garrick closed his eyes and slumped back in the chair. Even in the dark he felt the room swim. One tot of JB and he was almost out for the count. Howard's voice kept him focused.

"You're too close to this, David. Don't you see who's the distraction? You." Garrick opened his eyes. Howard was now leaning forward with his elbows on the table. His voice lowered, forcing Garrick to tune out the background noise. "If this circus has come to town for you, then you're the one who shouldn't be here."

Garrick nodded in agreement. Howard sighed and rapped the table with his knuckles. Garrick caught the flash of a wedding ring.

"Problem is, it would be mighty dumb of me to let you

and *your* circus just go back home. Not until I have some answers."

"There will be no answers, Sergeant. Only more questions."

WHEN SERGEANT HOWARD dropped Garrick back at the motel, he noticed the Ford Explorer was in the parking lot. Falling snow had already obliterated the tyre tracks, and he wondered if they would be able to do film anything tomorrow. He considered knocking on Molly's door to tell her what had happened, but exhaustion was sapping his resolved. It was late, and for all he knew the crew may have staggered off to a bar. Besides, the first set-up was supposed to be interviewing Sergeant Howard at the station. How were these new developments going to affect that?

His room key was stiff in the lock, but he opened it on the third try. The alcohol was clashing with jet lag, and he almost tripped as he entered the room. Inside wasn't much warmer than out. The air from the electric fan heater under the window was asthmatic. He turned the yellowing plastic dial up and shucked off his coat. He barely had the presence of mind to connect his phone to the charger before he stripped down to his underwear and folded himself under the sheets.

Sleep came instantly.

8

8

GARRICK WOKE WITH A JOLT. His brain was wreathed in fog as he tried to separate his dream from reality. A light from the floor focused his attention. Wendy's name flashed up on an incoming FaceTime call, but the phone was on silent. Garrick reached for it, but it must have fallen from the bed as it lay just out of reach. He swung his body over the edge of the bed and stretched. It was a monumental feat. His limbs felt sore, and his head pounded. By the time he reached the phone the screen turned black. He tapped it, but nothing happened. The battery was dead again.

With a grunt of effort, Garrick twisted around so he could sit upright in the dark room. He put his head in his hands and gently massaged his temples. He was still fully dressed. He'd only had one drink, yet he was nursing the mother of hangovers. His only thought was to charge his phone and call Wendy straight back.

Then a rational part of his mind cried out for attention. The phone was on silent, so that couldn't have woken him. He recalled a loud sound in his dream. Something breaking... something heavy. Had he been plagued by a nightmare that had roused him?

Flickering light from the motel sign outside played through the window. It was still night time, and the room was stifling warm. His mouth felt dry, and he smacked his lips still tasting the JB he'd drank earlier. Gauging the quality of the motel's bathroom, he didn't particularly want to drink the water. He recalled a vending machine outside the manager's office. His coat was crumpled on the table where he'd left it. Patting the pocket to check his wallet was inside, he put it on, made sure he had his key, and stepped outside.

The surging storm stung his face the moment he stepped onto the veranda. He bowed his head against the breeze and pulled his door closed. The bitter cold helped clear his head a little, but he still felt groggy as he stumbled down the flight of steps to the ground floor. Just how drunk was he?

The light from the vending machine beckoned him towards the manager's office. Snow was already piling against one side of the machine. With each step, Garrick felt an uncomfortable prickle run down his spine. Not from the cold, but from the copper's sixth sense that had saved him from so many predicaments in the past.

He paused and looked around the lot. Everything was quiet. Even traffic was absent from the street. No cars had passed for some time, judging by the thin layer of snow settling across the asphalt. He fumbled for his wallet, extracting a pair of dollars from the vending machine that was stocked with Gatorade, Coke, and an assortment of energy drinks. A coke it would have to be. He raised the notes to the payment slot – and then froze.

His fingers were stained with blood.

He quickly flexed his hand, searching for a cut, but it wasn't his. It had dried, but the wet snow on his fingers liquified it again. Then two thoughts hit him at once. He spun around, scanning the parking lot for his crew's Ford Explorer. It wasn't there. Then he turned back to the manager's office as a detail his foggy mind hadn't initially registered was now nagged him for attention. The glass in the door was smashed. Not enough to shatter it completely, but enough to cover it in a web of impact lines that turned it opaque. The door was also ajar by a couple of inches.

The breath caught in Garrick's throat as he took the few steps to the door and pushed. Something was blocking it inside. He pressed his shoulder against the doorframe and pushed. The door begrudgingly opened, pushing a weight behind it. He created just enough space to step inside.

The office had been ransacked. From the look of it, a botched robbery. The manager's desk had been overturned, the computer smashed, and papers cast everywhere. All of it was covered in blood. The manager himself lay behind the door, a fire axe protruding from his skull. The blade had been brought down with such force there was a wedge of bone and brain matter missing, and the corner of the axe had embedded in the wooden floor below.

The entire room spun around Garrick, and he felt himself falling. The smell of blood, usually so familiar, now made his stomach turn. The loose dollars in his hand dropped to the floor as he staggered. Supporting himself against the wall was the only way he stopped himself from dropping.

"Think!" he snapped at himself.

He saw the landline telephone had fallen from the desk; the handset stained by fresh blood. His impulse was to call the police, but caution prevented him from doing so. Everything about this jarred him. The blood on his hands. The crime scene around him. The hangover. Had he been drugged in the bar? He tried to recall faces of the other patrons, but his concentration refused to stay fixed. A sudden flurry of red lights outside confirmed the doubt brewing within. The police had arrived with no prompt the public.

He was being set up.

Every rational voice in his head told him to wait and submit to the approaching law enforcement, but their pleas were overshadowed by a cautious undertow: who could be trusted? Who would listen to him? So far, he hadn't been spotted...

His eyes darted to a fire door leading to the rear of the property. He suddenly found a second wind of energy as he hurried over and used his thigh to press against the bar. It opened smoothly, and he slipped outside, quietly closing the door behind.

The rear of the motel was protected from the wind, so the snow had yet to settle here. Instead, the concrete floor was dry and allowed him quick access past half a dozen wheeled dumpsters, as he circled around the longest leg of the U-shaped building. It took him out close to the street, away from the police cruiser that had pulled up. He was just in time to see the uniformed officer stagger out of the office and throw up next to a bush before using his radio to call in the crime.

Garrick's stomach churned as he tried to focus on the scene. A task made even more difficult by a gnawing headache. He needed space to think and recover. Pulling his jacket tightly closed and shoving his hands deep into his pockets, Garrick hurried quickly away.

And with each step he knew he was miring himself into deeper trouble.

AT FIRST GLANCE, the wall of problems appeared insurmountable. While Flora was designated as a 'city' in the US, Garrick's British notion of what that represented was vastly different. With a population of little over four thousand, it didn't even qualify as a town back in the UK. And it was effectively cut off by flat, exposed farmland in every direction, which meant few places to lie low, making it a difficult place to leave unnoticed. Even before his visit, Garrick had digested every fact and memorised the entire area as he delved into his sister's death.

His idea that the United States was a bustling twenty-four-hour culture was struck dead when he realised there wasn't any diner open. There was nowhere to buy a warm coffee to sober himself up. Instead, he found himself hunkered out of the storm in the back lot of business park on the edge of town. He stole warmth from a power generator, which sounded alarmingly loud and on the verge of exploding. At least it kept the cold at bay.

He'd taken his wallet with him, containing one-hundred twenty-four dollars, and his mobile phone, which was out of power. He'd left his passport back in his room.

He re-ran the events in his mind's eye. He hadn't imbibed enough to be this drunk, he was sure of that. He'd suffered blackouts and hallucinations before, that was on his medical record and something he suspected would be used against him. He couldn't recall what time Sergeant Howard had dropped him back at the motel as jet lag had swamped him. The inky blackness around him offered no hint of the current time. His only conclusion was that he'd been drugged. Either at the bar or somebody had entered his room.

Which meant he was being set up for sure.

The only culprit what made any sense were the dregs from the Murder Club. The deliberate slaying of another David Garrick confirmed elements were still in play, and they could be entrenched in any strata of society. His first instinct was to cast suspicion on Sergeant Howard. The officer had been in his life since the moment his sister had died. He was the ineffectual lead on the investigation until the FBI had taken it over, and he was the last person Garrick had been with.

Yet he wasn't convinced. He hoped he wasn't being biased towards another member of law enforcement. God knew the club had its tendrils there, too. It also left the issue that Howard was his *only* suspect, which was ridiculous.

What was also ridiculous was how everything felt so deliberately engineered. The recent David Garrick victim, designed to be found so Garrick could find him as he was standing next to *Howard*. The same name as the leader of the Murder Club who had put him through a hell that was contrived to mess with his mind for reasons he still couldn't fathom.

The logical thing to do was walk into the police precinct and talk to Howard. It may not look good that he wasn't there right now, but there was no reason for him not to be honest...

Except there was blood on his hands. Literally. Where had that come from? He felt queasy. If he had been drugged, then the killer must have set that up. If that was the case, what else had been planted? Had he touched anything in the office? He'd interacted with the door to enter and the fire escape. If he hadn't used his hands, then he knew forensics well enough to know his coat would have left fibres on the door.

And the dollars he'd prepared for the vending machine... he riffled his pockets. They were not there. He'd dropped them in the crime scene. The ones with his bloody prints on.

That didn't look innocent. He certainly wouldn't look upon circumstances positively it if he were leading the investigation. He needed more grit on his side. He couldn't rely purely on circumstantial evidence. He should contact Molly... but of course, that's the first contact he'd be expected to make, and she wasn't back at the motel, which raised questions about why. Without knowing the time, it was difficult to even guess where she could have gone. The final detail was the police arriving just in time. That was no fluke.

He wasn't naive enough to think he could solve everything on his own, but the first step was to prove his innocence. Perhaps it was the drugs circulating his system, or the sense of panic coursing through him, but Garrick knew he would have to do the unthinkable.

He'd have to become a fugitive.

9

DAWN, and David Garrick wore a thick quilted jacket that provided better warmth than his Barbour. He'd taken it from the back of an old pickup truck he'd broken into and, with some effort, hot-wired. Fortunately, the vehicle was so old he could do so. A modern vehicle would have thwarted him.

He'd driven the pickup out of town, and through a stretch of snowbound highway westbound towards St Louis, the biggest city in the vicinity and that was one hundred miles away. After twenty miles, the snow cleared, and he u-turned back into Flora and hid the vehicle close to where he'd stolen it, amongst dense foliage in what he hoped would be the last place anybody would look. On the surface, it was a dumb plan, but he was hoping he'd achieved enough to give the impression he'd left town.

With little he could do to disguise his appearance, other than firmly pull down a grubby baseball cap that had been in the pickup and smelled of sweat and oil, Garrick returned as close as he could to the crime scene. It was still snowing, but now it came down in sporadic gentle bursts as he reached the Motel.

Police tape blocked access to the parking lot, and an array of police vans were already parked. There was no sign yet of a CSI team, which potentially gave him more time on the run. A dozen uniformed cops kept a growing crowd of people at bay, most of whom were filming on the cell phones. A local TV news van had caught the scent of the story and was hurriedly setting up the camera. Garrick spotted a grim-faced Sergeant Howard emerging from the office, deep in conversation with another officer. Howard indicated the motel's block of rooms, which Garrick noted had yet to be evacuated.

He was too far away to hear anything useful and dared not get closer. He scanned the parking lot for Molly's van. It wasn't there. He wasn't sure what to make of that - relief that she wasn't yet caught up in this new loop of madness, or concern that the team appeared to be missing? He knew one thing for sure: the audacity of the Murder Club members knew no limits. They were meticulous planners, so he knew every contingency and every *person* in Garrick's immediate vicinity had been factored in.

He had to think outside the constraints of what would be expected of him. He watched as a white truck was waved through the police cordon and parked close to the office. Doctor Dugu, wearing a thick green jacket, climbed out and made straight for Howard. Garrick tried to put himself in Howard's shoes. With no CSI team, and possibly quite a wait if it had to come from St Louis, he presumed Doctor Dugu had been called on site to help preserve the crime scene.

There was no way Garrick could get closer to the motel or extract any useful information from here. For now, those clues would remain beyond his reach. He'd have to start elsewhere to get a handle on the killer. Information in the police station was inaccessible. But with Dugu here, he reasoned that the coroner's office should be empty.

GARRICK WAS thankful that Flora possessed a small-town mentality. The alarm on the coroner's office emergency door still hadn't been fixed and was easy enough to jemmy open with a piece of broken fencing rail that had been discarded behind the building. He carefully wiped the rail clean of prints before tossing it into the undergrowth and then entered the dark corridor.

He paused to listen for any signs that Maureen was at work, but guessed it was far too early for her shift. Satisfied he was alone, Garrick turned the lights on with his elbow and padded across to the mortuary. Using only the light from the corridor, he took in the room. Dugu diligently kept it clean and fastidiously tidy, but Garrick spotted a metal trolly with implements carefully lined up next to a box of blue latex gloves. He headed straight for them. Slipping a pair on, he stuffed several more in his pocket for later use. Feeling a little more confident he wouldn't be leaving a trail of prints, Garrick turned the lights on and moved to the computer on a desk in the corner. Wiggling the mouse, it woke from sleep, straight to the desktop.

No password, Garrick smiled to himself, thankful for the lax security.

The computer's clock said it was 8:13am. That at least helped put his day in perspective. The medical reporting program was still open. A few mouse clicks and it filled the screen. He clicked on the search box. It felt eerie to type his own name. Hitting the enter key called up the doctor's report. He still hadn't finished typing it up, so it hadn't yet been sent to the police.

A series of gruesome photos filled the gallery. Close ups of the various wounds taken against a ruler for scale. Garrick had seen countless similar images, and without an expert's notation there was little he could read into the wounds. The doctor's report was lengthy, with many highlighted passages where he intended to add further details. His wording bordered just beyond clinical professionalism, with a definite thrill towards the sadistic care and intricacies the killer had attained. In some parts, it felt like reading the transcript of a true crime podcast.

Garrick drilled into the finer nuances. The precision stitching and scalpel work on the victim hinted the killer had medical training beyond that of a student, noting 'hidden stitches.' There were a few traces of borax that had been used to persevere the skin, but nothing on the construction of the tank or general details about the crime scene, which would be the remit of the CSI team. Garrick felt a twinge of disappointment. He didn't know what details he may have stumbled over, but there was scant information here to help him take a positive step in any direction. He noted the case file number and put the computer back to sleep. With a last look around the room, he turned the lights off and closed the door behind him.

He took a step towards the rear door, then stopped. He turned and continued to the front of the building and found

Maureen's reception desk, complete with paper-filled in-trays. Garrick sat down, glad that she was the sort of person resistant to change. Good old paperwork left a much more tangible trail. For once, luck was with him. The case notes David Garrick lay on the top tray.

The man was fifty-three, divorced and lived in Springfield, which he recalled was somewhere to the north. He'd been reported missing for two weeks, but it had been noted he'd turned to alcohol during the divorce, so no suspicious circumstances were flagged. Garrick checked the date of the report. The hairs on his arm rose. It was a day after his flight to the US had been confirmed. The poor guy had probably been targeted for some time, unknowingly with a death sentence over his head. One that would be executed the moment DCI David Garrick confirmed he was travelling to the States.

His mind wrapped around these additional facts. Molly had confirmed the trip with him and Kamila the same day. The same day he had handed in his travel dates to his Super so the times could be blocked off the station's rota. It was a safe bet that either Molly or Kamila would have confirmed the dates with Sergeant Howard, too. He couldn't recall when he was told Scott came onboard, but something told him that was more recent. This gave the killer a small pool of collaborators. Unfortunately for Garrick, they extended across two continents, and he was confined to this town.

He needed to create options.

If he could get in touch with his team back home, they could investigate any leaks in Molly's inner circle. Of course, his Super will soon be more than aware of his current circumstances and would be obliged to let Flora PD know he'd made contact. The only person who could buck the rules would be DC Fanta Liu, but contacting her would place her in an unenviable position. One that might harm her career.

Garrick took his phone out to take pictures of the file, only to remember the battery was dead. He extracted several sheets of blank paper from the printer and began writing the late David Garrick's details: his home address, that he was a business owner although it didn't state his profession, and contact details for his ex-wife. As he did so, vague recollections about US law popped to mind. If he was to get out of State, it would help his chance of keeping under the police radar. There seemed to be a communication problem between forces... or was that something that only existed in TV shows? As he copied the details down, he mulled crossing west in Missouri, where he could get lost in St Louis. Or Indiana and Kentucky were close by to the east.

He stopped and stared at the town he had just written: Springfield. That's where the victim was from. North of Flora, it meant it was within the same State. A missing persons case and subsequent murder was a big story, but if it didn't cross a state line, then it was a local matter, not the FBI's jurisdiction. Had the killer taken that into consideration? If so, it would have taken a lot of effort to locate another Garrick in Illinois. The killer must have spent a reasonable about of time there...

David Garrick stared at the notes he made, then reached a decision. He needed to find a point of entry into the crime trail to jump onboard and forge his own clues. He needed to go to Springfield.

Decision made, he folded his notes and slipped them into the inside pocket of his coat. He returned the victim's file into the in-tray and stood up, checking he'd left nothing out of place. Satisfied, he turned the lights off and hurried down the dark corridor towards the backdoor.

He was halfway along when he heard the front door open. There was a rattle of keys and the sound of the door closing. Maureen must have come into work. Garrick froze, only a few metres from escape. His last steps would be through a squeaking door. Was Maureen's hearing poor? Could he make it without her noticing?

With little choice, Garrick padded to the door, intending on making a hasty escape. He put a hand on the handle... then hesitated. Whoever had entered the office hadn't turned the light on. There came sounds of something heavy moving. The dull thump was broken by the sound of pouring liquid.

Garrick removed his hand from the door and took a step back. He heard the front door open again – and with it came a breeze from outside carrying with it the distinctive smell of petrol.

A second later, an enormous orange fireball exploded in the reception office. The air sucked past him, down the corridor, fuelling the explosion with a backdraught. Seconds later, a wall of heat struck him – and he shouldered through the back door.

10

1o

GARRICK COULD ONLY WATCH HELPLESSLY as the flames rapidly spread across the coroner's office. The snow was falling hard again, and a breeze washed the thick black smoke across the street. In an area of town surrounded by shops and bars, he was unsure if anybody would be around to report the blaze, and he could hardly do it himself. One thing was certain, he couldn't afford to hang around.

Garrick slipped off the blue gloves, which looked out of place for somebody taking a stroll down the street. He bowed his head against the storm and hurried away.

He made it to the pickup he'd concealed as he heard the first sounds of a fire engine. That was a good few minutes' delay, more than enough time for the fire to gut the office. As he climbed into the cab, he ran what had happened through his mind's eye. The arsonist had targeted the front office, not the rest of the facility, which indicated the target wasn't the corpse but the medical records. But why target those? They were mere copies that Maureen had handed over when Garrick and Howard were in the room. It made no sense.

The ignition's stripped ignition cables sparked as he twisted them together, and the engine ticked over. He smoothly drove out of Flora, resisting the urge to drive faster. He passed another fire engine and police car speeding towards the fire, and onto the forty-five he'd originally entered town on. Other than heading north, he didn't have a sat-nav on which to plot his path. He'd have to rely on old-fashioned road signs.

It was more than likely the fire wasn't coincidental. Which meant the culprit was in on the killings. He wrestled with the idea of returning, hating that he'd been so close to the villain – but was now heading away from them. It was an act of sabotage that he was sure Sergeant Howard would pin on him, so that further increased the need to leave town. However, it also meant that his ruse to trick the authorities that he'd headed to St Louis in the dead of night may well have been a waste of time and the vehicle he was in risked police attention. He just had to make sure he drove sensibly – not too wild, and certainly not too cautiously. Cars driving too far under the speed limit and acting too perfectly were often telltale signs that the driver was either drunk or stoned and trying too hard.

The weather remained a constant flurry of snow. The ploughs had been out in force, so the road was clear. However, the straight roads, constant weather, and bland landscape became hypnotic, and Garrick felt the lack of sleep wearing him down. A signpost directed him onto the 185 and he soon found a fuel stop where he could park to the side and snatch some sleep.

Without an alarm, he woke just over two hours later. A veil of snow covered the windshield, and the cab was chilly enough to reveal his breath. It took him some moments to get his brain up to speed. The dash clock read 13:32pm. The last sign he'd seen put Springfield seventy miles away, so his ETA would be late afternoon. What he was planning to do there remained a mystery.

His stomach rumbled, reminding him that the last time he'd eaten was over twenty-four hours earlier. He'd have to risk buying something in the gas station. A truck and two cars were refuelling, but the weather was keeping general traffic at bay. Inside, a bored teenage clerk had his nose him his phone. Behind him, a TV played various commercials for dog food, health insurance and gardening equipment. Garrick headed straight for the coffee machine and navigated the touchscreen to make him a twelve-ounce black coffee. He hated caffeine. It never agreed with his stomach, but he needed something to keep him going. He selected four unfamiliar chocolate bars and a bean burrito, which he placed in the customer microwave, and set it for two minutes.

All the while he kept his eye on the forecourt outside. One driver entered to buy a bag of chips and a soda as an SUV arrived and the soccer mom driving headed straight inside to pay for her fuel before it was dispensed.

Once the customers left, he took the burrito from the microwave. It was scalding hot, so he used a bunch of paper towels to insulate his hand. As he did, he noticed the television was running the local news. With ironic timing, the presenter of the local news team he'd seen setting up outside the motel was now delivering her report. It was muted, so Garrick garnered no extra details. His stomach knotted as he waited for his photo to appear, but it didn't come. Instead, the news rolled on to a story about a car crash. He felt a twinge of relief and crossed to the counter. The clerk was in no mood to make small talk, which suited Garrick. He peeled off fifteen dollars, then on impulse bought a USB iPhone charging cable hanging on the end of the counter.

Back in the pickup he devoured the burrito, savouring the warmth. He sipped the bitter coffee and winced as his stomach gurgled as it soaked up the caffeine. For some reason, his mugshot wasn't circulating, so that gave him some hope he was a step ahead.

He pulled the cable ties off the charging cable and plugged one end into his iPhone. He held the USB plug over the cigarette lighter. There was no USB socket. The pickup was far too old to have one.

"Dammit..." he muttered.

He needed his phone to contact Molly, Fanta, and Wendy – the latter who must be fretting that he hadn't called home since he arrived. Then he realised what a lucky break he'd had. Turning his phone on would have led the authorities straight to him. For a first-time criminal, it was a rookie mistake. He had to think logically.

Taking a gulp of coffee, he started the pickup and headed towards Springfield.

EIGHTY MINUTES LATER, Garrick drove into the city limits of Springfield. He had expected it to be a clone of Flora, but a grand sign welcomed him to the State Capital. As he crossed a bridge over a picturesque lake, complete with a petite lighthouse, and turning off the highway, he found himself in the usual American grid pattern of streets, except these were of wooden panelled homes that looked quintessentially American to Garrick's eyes. Each one was far bigger than he could hope to afford back home and, nestled in the snow, they looked quaint and wholesome. A few minutes later he was on 2nd Street and driving past well persevered colonial buildings which gave way to the magnificent domed State Capitol building.

Aware he was now driving aimlessly, and it was going to be much more difficult to track down an individual than he'd supposed, Garrick took a right when he saw a coffee shop. Intending to hunker down there, he searched for a parking spot. The area seemed busy with a mixture of suits and students. Several passing patrol cars worried him, further encouraging him to ditch the pickup. Then he spotted a sign for the Lincoln Library. Even better, it had underground parking. Garrick pulled in and found a spacious spot to leave the pickup.

Aware his stolen cap and grimy jacket made him look more like a local hick, he pocketed the cap and swapped back into his Barbour. Spitting into his palm, he slicked back his tousled hair.

His gaunt, stubbled expression held his gaze.

What had he done to deserve this ordeal?

He pocketed the uneaten candy bars, his phone and charging cable, and left the vehicle without the intention to return. The library was a pleasant modern building, filled with students and locals keen on escaping the snow outside. Garrick forced himself to walk with casual confidence, although the caffeine was turning his stomach into knots, and he desperately needed to use a bathroom.

He found a bank of computers and slipped into the seat as an elderly man stood up to leave. He navigated to his Gmail account, but hesitated from logging in. He seldom used his personal account and was unsure what alarms would be triggered if he logged into it now. Years being a detective had shown him the many ways evidence could be built against a suspect. He had learned that there was no single compromising clue that led the authorities to a criminal. Digital footprints tended to be the best to follow. He also knew that a lot of real-time tracing techniques that cops used in TV shows belonged more in the realms of James Bond more than it did the real world. Even if he was being surveilled by the CIA, they'd struggle to lock his location down at this present time.

He logged into his email account. A quick scan through revealed no messages of interest, and quite a lot of spam. He quickly messaged Wendy, saying he'd lost his phone. He did not know if she had yet been approached by the police back home, probably not, but that would only be a matter of time. He added that he was okay, then added a vague hint that she shouldn't worry.

His second email went to DC Fanta Liu. He drafted three versions of the message, deleting each in turn. He wanted to give her details and ask for help, but he knew that could incriminate her if she helped. Instead, he opted for a series of blunt sentences:

BEING SET UP. THEY ARE STILL ACTIVE. DON'T KNOW WHO TO TRUST.

.   .   .

THE LAST SENTENCE was rather melodramatic, but he was certain she'd get the point to be cautious and knew she'd read into it he wanted her to monitor Wendy. As he clicked on send, he wasn't sure what help she could offer, if any. However, he felt a slight weight off his chest, knowing he wasn't alone with his knowledge, even if it felt like it. As added security, he deleted the sent emails, and ensured they were erased from his *deleted items* folder too. In the past, he'd had to deal with requests to access data from these digital giants. They were always very uncooperative. Eager to protect the privacy of their users, even if they were criminals. For once, Garrick was thankful for their attitude.

Next, he searched for *David Garrick, Springfield.* The first few hits were freshly posted state-wide news articles about his death. Nobody seemed to have any details, so they were pithy stories that just filled space in the news cycle. Another innocent victim who would be forgotten by the masses; nothing more than a few paragraphs in anybody's day.

While most of the articles appeared to be cut-and-paste jobs from a police press release, one near the bottom of the list was worded differently enough to attract Garrick's attention. It was from a local Springfield newspaper and contained a few more details, citing the victim as estranged from his family and combatting alcohol addiction. There was also a reference to his job as a taxidermist.

Alarm bells rang in Garrick's head.

Another quick Google search brought up the victim's taxidermy premises to the west of the city. Checking an online map, he added to the notes he'd made in the coroner's office. It was just over an hour's walk, but he felt that was a better option than risking using the pickup again. Pausing only to clear his browsing history, Garrick left the library with the scent of his quarry luring him onwards.

11

1 *I*

ETERNAL TAXIDERMY WAS a single-story retail unit close to a Walgreens supermarket. A wire mesh across the window and another mesh door across the front door provided physical security. Garrick peered through the window at a small ginger cat and Labrador dog, impeccably preserved and posed as if they were the best if friends. Garrick wasn't a pet-person, but he still liked animals. He couldn't understand why somebody would want their deceased furry pal gazing back at them from across the room. He could only imagine the trauma that would cause a child.

A dirty white alarm box over the door flashed a white light to ward potential thieves away. Glancing around the parking lot, Garrick saw a couple of cameras on other store front premises, all pointing to their own doorways. He couldn't see any cameras covering the parking area. Living in the UK, he'd become accustomed to some of the highest levels of surveillance in the world. Over here, on the surface at least, it felt far less draconian.

He walked around the side of a beauty parlour on the corner and pretended to relieve himself. Luckily, during his brisk walk across the city he had sought refuge in a Starbucks toilet as his stomach cramps increased. The small cubicle had its own sink, which he took advantage of to clean himself. It had cost him almost ten dollars to buy a bottle of water and a muffin to use the facilities, but the food was welcome. The pantomime of taking a leak behind the building allowed him to check for security cameras. There were reenforced fire escapes down the side, but he couldn't see any cameras.

Now he was presented with a dilemma. The shop offered the only access he had into the victim's world. He'd looked up some books about taxidermy while in the library and discovered techniques for 'hidden stitches.' The same as indicated on the coroner's report. While it wasn't exclusively damning evidence, it was too close to ignore. He had little choice but to pursue the only lead he had, which meant breaking into the shop. The rear doorway was a solid steel slab, flush to the brickwork and designed only to be opened from the inside. So the front was the only way in.

As far as he could gauge, it was between five and six in the evening, and the sky was already dark enough to trigger the streetlights. The snow had stopped, but few people had ventured out on shopping expeditions. A quick glance at the opening hours of the surrounding stores indicated they would be shutting soon. Only the regular traffic in and out of Walgreens would continue until late. Luckily, that was several hundred yards away, so he guessed his actions wouldn't attract attention from there. He could wait until after midnight, but wasn't sure if that offered him much of an advantage. If he triggered an alarm and had to flee, wandering through the city after midnight would rouse more attention than early evening when people were still returning from work or heading out for the night.

While there were many questions vying for attention, he focused on the most immediate problem — how to break in. The cage across the door was locked with a single new padlock, while the window mesh was held in place by two of them. Once through the door cage, no doubt the door would be locked too, but two large opaque glass windows would easily break, allowing entry.

He needed some tools. He recalled passing a hardware store next to his favourite Starbucks. He hurriedly retraced his steps, hoping to make it before closing time. Mindful of his dwindling budget, and knowing that using his credit card, like his phone, would attract attention by anybody looking for him, he paid in cash for a roll of gaffer tape, a heavy hammer, a screwdriver, and a small flashlight he could slip into his pocket.

Upon returning to the taxidermy store, he was relieved to see the other stores had closed. While some of their signs were illuminated, many were dark. Only the lights across the parking lot provided any immediate illumination, and luck was with him – Eternal taxidermy lay just beyond the reach of the light.

Checking there was nobody around, Garrick set about opening the caged screen. Slipping on a pair of latex gloves, he studied the door. Rather than attack the padlock directly, he'd noticed the hinges were made from steel pins hammered through the metal wall brackets. During his time walking the beat as a regular copper, he'd attended many burglaries and witnessed a wide assortment of techniques. One he'd seen a couple of times might prove useful now.

Positioning the tip of the screwdriver against the central pin on the lower hinge, Garrick struck it firmly with the hammer. The cold was numbing his fingers, and his aim was off. The screwdriver jolted from his hand. He scrambled to pick it up as it rolled towards a gaping drainage hole where the sidewalk met the parking lot.

He tried again, taking more care to line up his aim. The first hit was on target, but lacked any real force. He tried again and was rewarded with a trickle of dust from the hinge. Garrick repeated the motion again and again, and with each strike the pin raised upward. After seven attempts, the pin finally popped from the hinge and rolled across the floor.

Who would have thought being a criminal was so satisfying? Garrick thought to himself as he set about extracting the top bolt. The pin jumped out on his third strike, and Garrick caught it before it hit the ground.

With the hinges removed, it was straightforward to open the cage the opposite way around; the padlock acting as an improvised hinge. The next step was the glass. Arguably the easiest, but the one most likely to catch people's attention. Garrick covered the bottom panel with a layer of gaffer tape, taking care to ensure the entire surface was covered. It was snowing again when he finished. Kneeling, he used the hammer to lightly, but firmly break the glass along the edge of the frame. With each impact, it broke, but the tape held it in place. Within a minute, he could lift the entire taped panel into the shop beyond. Now he had an obvious entry point. He looked around one last time. Regular traffic was passing down the street. A bus filled with people drove past. Distant shoppers visited Walgreens, but nobody looked in his direction.

David Garrick crawled into the taxidermy store. He had feared there would be motion sensors inside, triggering the alarm... but nothing sounded. He supposed it could be a silent alarm, calling the local security company at that very moment, but those were not cheap systems, and he was gambling it was beyond the budget of a taxidermist.

He propped the broken gaffer-taped glass panel up to cover the hole in the door and stood to examine the store. It was pitch black, so he was glad to have the foresight to buy the flashlight. To one side was a shelving unit filled with stuffed critters – from birds to squirrels. The shadows cast by the flashlight seemed to make them dance. It was rather macabre.

A wooden counter was home to a cash register and an assortment of mounts, stands, and plaques. It blocked access to the back room, which was partitioned by a thick curtain. Garrick drew it back and entered the second room.

This was where his namesake conducted his business. A central table was covered with tools: blades, scissors, hacksaws, sewing materials, while the surrounding shelves had an assortment of chemicals in plastic containers, including formaldehyde and borax. Several large chest freezers ran along the back wall, near the fire escape.

Garrick took it all in, wondering where to search for clues that may help him prove his innocence. Several large knives lay on the draining board, next to a deep corner sink. A box of black tea and a jar of sugar sat in the corner, next to a hot water dispenser. In the sink were a pair of cups and a spoon. It looked as if the owner had just left for the day, intending to return to work the following morning...

Which made him wonder why the police hadn't been here yet. It had been two weeks since Garrick #2 had been reported missing, and only a day since discovering his body. With the store being locked from the outside and no signs of a struggle through the window, it was a good bet the police wouldn't force entry, which meant he was ahead of the curve.

He opened the nearest refrigerator and recoiled at the face of a Doberman. It took a few seconds for his heart to stop racing as he realised it was somebody's poor pet due to become a piece of furniture. He quickly closed the door and moved to the next refrigerator. His hand was on the handle when he paused and turned to the sink.

Two cups.

Curious, he lifted one out and angled his flashlight around it. There was a distinctive lipstick mark on the rim. Garrick couldn't imagine he'd bring a customer back to the cutting room. The relationship with his ex-wife was volatile and there had been no mention of children. Did he have an assistant? If so, *she* wasn't referred to in the press articles. The wounds and careful stitching used to mount him as a display required a great deal of skill – something an assistant or fellow taxidermist would also have...

He cast his torch around the room. Had he been murdered here? It was quite an assumption to make, but why not? All the tools were at hand. And killed by a woman he worked with and trusted...

Garrick struggled to make sense of his thoughts. Fatigue was once again gnawing at him. He had to concentrate, to be alert for the smallest of clues, but his mind was fudge. He needed to rest and, despite his revulsion, this was the warmest place he'd find. It couldn't yet be nine in the evening, so even a huge six-hour sleep would allow him plenty of time to conduct a thorough search in the dead of night. It was too good an opportunity to miss.

He found an electric heater in the corner and turned it on. He had to stop operating on jet lag and fatigue. If he was going to make any progress, he needed to be at the peak of his game. He lay in front of the heater and folded his Barbour into a pillow. As the warm air caressed his skin, he swore he felt Wendy's soft touch across his cheek, and the smell of her natural scent flared his nostrils as he fell asleep...

1 ²

A TERRIBLE THROBBING pain in Garrick's temples jarred him awake. With it came an intense, nauseous feeling. It was too dark to see anything, and he felt weak all over, as if he'd been struck down by a sudden flu.

He tried to recall his last few moments exploring the taxidermy back room. It would be clumsy of the assailant to leave any clues that would connect them to the murder of his alter ego, but his hunch that there was an assistant involved spoke to the suspicious copper inside him. Had they befriended the American taxidermist and learned from his skill set with the sole intention of butchering him the moment DCI Garrick arrived in the US to follow the trail of his sister's killer? It certainly fit within the sadistic *modus operandi* the Murder Club had established. Murder for sport.

Garrick was suddenly jolted. Alarmed, he raised his head – and it slammed against something hanging above him. He stretched, his legs and arms hitting the enclosing walls.

He wasn't in the store.

Frantic, he rolled onto his back. His hands ran along the ceiling that was just a foot or so overhead. He brushed the coarse carpet, the functional sort that would line the interior of a car boot. Only when he tried to move his hands further did he feel the cold metal of the cuffs binding them together. He'd been abducted, that was for sure. A swell of panic coursed through him, but he withheld the instinct to pound the roof and scream. He had to assess the situation.

There was no engine noise, so they were not moving. Had he just been loaded into the car, or was he at his destination? It was impossible to tell. The throbbing in his head indicated he'd been drugged, but he hadn't eaten or drank anything before sleeping. A gas perhaps?

Again, the vehicle jolted around him. They were moving. Silently. An electric car? That might limit the range. He scrunched his eyes tightly closed and opened them again, hoping they'd adjust to the dark – but the absolute absence of light continued. The glow-in-the-dark safety handle within the trunk, created for just this circumstance, was missing. Applying gentle pressure above didn't budge the trunk. He was trapped, and his only advantage was that his abductor didn't know he was awake.

Had this been the gang's game plan all along? Garrick had been in a similar predicament not so long ago, back in the UK. Even then, the threat to murder him had felt an anti-climax when seen in the context of the elaborate planning it had taken to get him to this point.

He'd been on several criminal psychological training

courses, designed to get in the mind of a killer. The only concrete thing he'd come away with was that everybody was different. There was no universal killer mindset.

The sound of metal brakes crunching against disk pads rumbled through the trunk; a sound normally drowned out by the engine but now enhanced by the silence of the electric motor. There was a slight motion as somebody shifted weight inside the car. Then he heard the driver's door shut and footsteps circled the vehicle. This was his moment of action – his only chance to take his captor by surprised.

But he had his doubts this was really the end of the line for him. Now, more than ever, he expected the puppet master would appear finally for their *coup de grâce*. Why go to all this trouble and remain a faceless figure? After constantly thwarting past operatives, he was certain the villain behind the scenes would want to finally prove he had outwitted the police detective. That much he was certain. Even psychotic killers had an ego to pamper.

The trunk's lock snapped, and the boot slowly rose open, revealing a moonlit sky, but no person. Garrick counted off the seconds, but still nobody appeared. From his vantage point, he could see the full moon was casting across a clear sky. Eventually, he sat up and looked around. There were fields covered in pristine snow that stretched to the distant, dark horizon. He strained to listen, but could hear nothing.

With his heart hammering in his chest, Garrick swung his legs out from the trunk and braced himself for a sudden attack.

None came.

Shifting himself forward, his feet pressed against a snowy gravel track, and he stood up. He emerged from the boot of a Tesla Model X, the moonlight playing over the dark blue, or possibly black, paintwork of a vehicle that looked brand new. His feet were un-tethered, so he could make a run for it. He was still fully dressed, and his abductor had thoughtfully slipped his Barbour back on before cuffing him with shackles that had a foot-long chain between the bracelets that afforded him some movement. Escape was something that his nemesis didn't think was relevant.

As he turned around to soak in the landscape, his heart skipped when the familiar doors of a large grain hangar filled his vision. They had parked outside the very ranch building his sister had escaped from. The door was open a fraction and a beckoning warm orange glow radiated from inside. He could see fresh footprints leading from the driver's door, circling the car before heading to the hangar.

Garrick knew how remote they were. Making it on foot in freezing temperatures would probably finish him off just as efficiently as a knife through the heart. While the whole situation had been contrived to make it seem as if he had a choice, the reality was he only had two: to play stubborn and wait for the killer to drag him inside, or to enter the killing floor himself.

THE LULLING warm hue inside the hanger emanated from a dozen large halogen lights suspected on long chains from the rafters. Each hissed and sizzled as it heated the frigid air circulating the room. Garrick slowly stepped over the threshold of the sliding door. He was in no rush to meet to inevitable violence that lay ahead, but nor was he experiencing any fear. That emotion had ebbed from him with each footstep and was replaced by anger and hatred for those who had taken to destroying his life; for those who had taken many lives, including that of his own innocent sister.

Several meters into the room, and there was still no sign of his abductor. He was braced for anything, but the blatant absence of a threat was eroding his sudden confidence.

All part of their little game, he told himself.

Halfway into the room he caught a movement from the far shadows where the conveyor passed through a large hatch and into the grain silo. He froze and squinted against the light. It wasn't a person; it was one of several hanging chains swaying back and forth. He was sure it hadn't been moving when he entered, and it was placed too far back for a breeze to catch it.

It was a lure. A pendulum beckoning him forward.

For a moment, Garrick considered heading back outside and making a run for it. There was no doubt the Tesla was beyond his skills to wire. The fields were flat, white, and bathed in moonlight so offered no cover. The temperature was far below freezing and the chances of encountering anybody else were negligible.

Onwards it was.

Garrick kept his eyes fixed on the hatchway ahead. Beyond, the darkness was thick, almost tangible. A mire that could conceal the most devious monster. Closer, he saw it was more of an opening cut into the wall where the raised conveyor belt continued onwards, with just enough clearance for a person to walk through if they shuffled sideways. The metal was rusting. The rubber matting brittle and peeling. Garrick sucked in his breath and crabbed through the gap, into the silo beyond.

1 ³

THE GENTLE SCRAPE of Garrick's handcuff chain along the metal side of the conveyor belt echoed tellingly in the circular silo tower beyond. Each footstep was amplified as he walked to the edge of the light pooling in behind him.

"So you got me here," he said, his voice croaking from his near muteness of the last day.

The last hissing syllables echoed around the chamber.

The lights faded up. Horizontal strips circled him, providing just enough illumination to light the bare central floor, and hinted at the corrugated iron walls that stretched to the darkness above.

A man stepped into the light opposite Garrick. Standing at six-four, he looked powerfully built under his bright yellow raincoat. His hair was slicked back, exposing high, almost feminine cheek bones. His skin was pale, which countered the fine red lipstick, which amplified his androgynous qualities. In his right hand, he casually swung a two-foot-long cattle prod.

He gave Garrick a star-struck smile and made a drumroll noise before raising his left hand, his fingers blossoming like a star. "Here he is in the flesh! Detective David Garrick. Wow!"

His flamboyant attitude startled Garrick. His eyes darted to-and-fro, this time noticing several small cylinders positioned under the lights. He couldn't be certain, but he suspected they were web-cameras. Which meant this idiot was performing to an audience.

"After all this charade, I only get to meet the monkey," Garrick said with a smirk. If they wanted a show, it wouldn't be one in which he trembled in fear.

The man's smile faltered. This wasn't the victim mentality he was used to. He stepped closer, raising the cattle prod between them. An electrical bolt crackled between the prongs. Garrick didn't flinch. At his core, he felt hollow. Beyond emotion. And, as his anger built, beyond empathy.

A flicker of irritation crossed the man's face. "I had expected better manners after everything I've heard." The man slowly circled around Garrick, looking him up and down as if for the first time. "Sadly, not everybody could be here for the grand finale." He made a vague gesture to the room.

"Mate. I don't give a shit." That made the guy stop in his tracks. Garrick smirked. "Oh, what's the matter? Does foul language upset your delicate sensibilities?"

That triggered the man. He stabbed the concrete floor twice with the prod. "Do you know how much effort has marshalled you to this point?" He sounded genuinely upset. "The amount of care and attention to detail that was all focused on you." He pointed the prod at Garrick, and the end sparked for emphasis.

"You're sick in the head. All of you."

The man shook his head. "No, Davy. No, we're not. Your mistake has always been that you saw this as a game. A game played out by some crazy psychopaths." His voice dropped to a hoarse whisper. "That's not true. You should think of this as an experiment in humanity."

Garrick's shoulders sagged, prompting the man to step closer.

"Your lot killed without discrimination. Then you brought my sister here and did God knows what to her. For no reason."

"That's not true. There was a reason for her to be here."

"So I'd end up following her trail to this very place?"

The man's smile returned, and he nodded. "Just how far can a person be pushed to walk down a deadly path to their own demise?" He gestured to the door. "You even walked in here of your own volition."

"That's because I intend to kill you," Garrick said in a low voice, his defeated gaze boring into the floor.

The man giggled. "See? I knew you were funny. An honest cop, too. One beyond corruption. One manipulated to cross the line and become what you hate. A felon. A man on the run. Can you now see what we created? A Frankenstein of the man you used to be! And, like a well-trained mutt, you followed every crumb I laid out to take you to that little store in Springfield."

Garrick was genuinely surprised. "You wanted me to go there?"

The man rolled his eyes. "You took your time. But it was the perfect place to snatch you. A little triazolam near the electric fire to KO you, and you were putty in my hands. After a little breaking and entering."

Garrick was puzzled. "Why?"

"You'd never find out, of course. But we have woven an elaborate web of incriminating evidence around yourself. For your legacy, you see." His brow furrowed when he saw Garrick's confusion. "Come on, you're smarter than this. Nobody is going to find your body here. Or anywhere else. You will vanish without a trace."

"Like you did with my sister?"

The man held up his hands. "I never touched your sister." His eyes narrowed. "She's not my type. What you will leave behind is your legacy. The mysterious player who has been manipulating everybody..." he pointed at Garrick. "The world is poised to see it's you. The orchestrater of your sister's death. The archangel behind the now defunct Murder Club. All brought down and exposed by whichever brave officer pieces together your trail. That's what we will have created. The greatest killer in history who masqueraded as an honest boy scout but was, in fact a merchant of death."

He took another step closer and raised the cattle prod.

Garrick wasn't listening to the monologue. He was too focused on the judgement call he had to make – how fast could be close the gap between the men? The prod was a close combat weapon, just like a knife. Reduce the distance between them and, like a blade, it could turn into a weapon that would harm the wielder. If they were touching, both Garrick and the psychopath would suffer.

"We created the ultimate piece of art." He gestured with both hands, as if presenting Garrick as a prize. "I wished I could've come to England myself. I would have had so much fun there, getting inside your head." He stepped closer and tapped the side of his skull. He was so focused on unburdening himself he didn't see Garrick tense.

And a second later, he didn't have time to react to Garrick springing forward.

Before making his move, Garrick had replayed his actions over-and-over in his head. His only weapon he had was the extended cuff chain. His statement about killing the man hadn't been hyperbole. It had been pure, raw intent. The conglomerate of murderers had indeed pushed him over the edge, but not into the world of a felon on the run. He was now prepared to be a killer. And like most premeditated killers, David Garrick relished the thought.

Mid-leap, Garrick crossed his forearms, aiming the chain for the man's throat. He flattened his chest to make him as broad as possible. He saw the cattle prod swing forward – but, as planned, he body-slammed into the man with his full mass. His assailant just had the edge on weight, but Garrick wasn't looking to knock him off his feet. It was enough that he couldn't swing the business end of the cattle prod into Garrick's skin. At the same time, he looped his right hand over the man's head – the chain circling his throat...

Then he uncrossed his arms with every ounce of power he had left. The chain snapped tight across the man's throat, and he heard cartilage snap and tear. The action had been so swift and precise, that only now gravity was asserting itself and he dropped. Which gave him another weapon.

The man was now yanked downward because of Garrick's full weight hanging from his throat. Garrick thrust his head towards the man's face and was rewarded with a splintering noise and a harsh impact on his forehead as he shattered the man's nose.

Garrick did not try to land safely. He didn't care if he broke his own bones in the assault. The sheer wild attack brought the man crashing down to the floor. Garrick felt his weight crush the breath out of him, but he didn't care. He didn't stop choking him.

The cattle prod clanged to the floor, feet away. Garrick tried to roll the man off, but he was too heavy.

"Die, you son of a–" Garrick was abruptly silenced as a punch struck his jaw. He heard a ringing noise in his skull and the silo wobbled around him. It was enough of a jolt to weaken him just enough. The man gripped Garrick's left hand and forced it back, just far enough to loosen the chain around his neck. The pressure increased on Garrick's clenched hand, and he experienced a sharp pain as a finger cracked.

Then the man rolled to the side and stretched for the cattle prod. His fingers closed around the insulated handle, and he stabbed to weapon down into Garrick's stomach. Garrick was fighting dirty now. Street rules. No holds barred. With his good hand, he grabbed the man's groin in a vice-like grip.

Just as the prod discharged 5600 volts into Garrick's stomach.

The pain was blinding, but he heard the man's high-pitched scream as a share of the current flowed through his testicles. The scent of burning cloth and flesh stung Garrick's nostrils, but there was nothing he could do about it. Every muscle in his body contracted with exquisite pain, and it felt like every nerve ending was on fire. White blotches, like multiple camera flashes, peppered his vision.

Garrick couldn't move. He could only watch as the man, with tears streaming down his cheeks, got to his knees. It took him a lot of effort to raise the cattle prod, but another strike was coming, and in his fragile state, Garrick wasn't sure he could withstand another jolt.

A woman's voice suddenly rang out. The words were slushed together. A series of letters that made no sense to Garrick.

Gunshots rang out.

1 ⁴

THE CLOCK WAS TICKING.

The pain in Garrick's abdomen stung every time he took a breath, but it was becoming so routine he now only felt it when he thought about it. He had to keep his mind occupied, which wouldn't be a problem.

"You're the face of this, David."

Even fastening the buttons of his shirt accentuated the painful cattle prod burn. His head still felt mush, so focusing on the woman's words was challenging as she continued.

"We have a narrow window of opportunity to bring this to a close. Do you understand?"

Garrick looked up at the Puerto Rican woman and managed a weak grin. "Despite your accent, you're doing well. You Americans will soon get the hang of English." The uncertainty crossing her face widened Garrick's smile.

"I'm sorry, but this is a serious matter–"

Garrick gestured to the cramped room around him. "Do you really have to tell me that?"

His smile dropped, and he studied the woman carefully. With long black hair pulled into a ponytail, and striking classic Puerto Rican features, she didn't look like the classic FBI agent – although with combat boots, cargo trousers, and an olive-green flak vest, she looked the part. The letters FBI stitched on her chest plate were also a terrific aide-memoire.

She had burst into the silo and shot Garrick's assailant twice in the leg and arm. Or so he'd been told. The gunshots and shouting had blended into a hazy cacophony as pain swamped him and he fell unconscious.

He woke in the medical room. An odd smell hung in the air as a uniformed paramedic dabbed the burnt flesh on his abdomen. Agent Adriana Rivera was the first clear face he saw. She had launched into a rapid explanation of what had happened, but it was too much for Garrick to digest at once. After an injection that woke him, Garrick finally realised he was being tended to in a veterinary surgery.

"We don't have time to take you to the hospital," Rivera said as she paced the room. "And you'd be too exposed."

"Exposed to who?"

Rivera stopped pacing as another agent entered and passed her a coffee. "Five minutes," he cautioned her. Rivera nodded and leaned against the windowsill as she addressed Garrick.

"We intercepted their web feed right at the start of their livestream–"

"That was being livestreamed?"

She waved her hand to stop him. "So as far as the rest of his crew are concerned, all is well, and you are dead."

"And that helps us, how? And that also begs the question why you didn't intervene earlier?"

Rivera's eyebrows raised in surprise. "Because you slipped our surveillance in Flora, and we didn't pick up on you until much later. The pickup you left at the library," she added, answering the question forming on his lips. "And getting a team in place was impossible before you were abducted."

"You didn't have eyes on the taxidermy shop?"

Rivera shook her head. "We had no clue. My guess is that piece of information was only in the coroner's office. I think they torched it to remove it, and to add an extra dimension to frame you."

"I have so many questions."

"And we have absolutely no time for them. David, you coming here was both a blessing and a nightmare."

"For whom?"

"Something tells me they would have got you here one way or another. I think the last-minute nature of the trip took them by surprise. They couldn't all be here."

"Have you identified them all?"

Rivera shook her head. "Grant is the first of them we've caught alive. Here at least." She picked up on his confused look. "Philip E. Grant. Your host back in the silo. I shot him in the arm and leg. He's alive, but not talking. I think he fears retribution if he opens his mouth. He was working with at least four others. We think they are the last of this group."

Garrick stared into space as his mind rushed to play catch up.

"And you have no identities?"

"Nope. We believe from cell phone activity that at least

one is still in Flora. They killed the motel owners and put your prints all over it."

"How do you know it wasn't me?"

Rivera arched an eyebrow. "Are you making a confession? I have to tell you, that would really screw things up."

"You don't have any leads on the identity of the others?"

"But I am betting you do."

Garrick looked curiously at her. "What makes you say that?"

Rivera smiled. "Before you go racing ahead here, I'm not making you an honorary FBI agent. This is America. You are a civilian. And that sort of thing only ever happens in schlocky movies."

"Noted."

"And technically, you fled the scene of a crime. At least twice. Stole a vehicle, so that's grand theft. And broke into two properties."

Garrick tucked his shirt into his waistband. "That's quite a conundrum. Especially because you are about to use me on a fishing expedition."

Rivera wagged a finger between them. "Great minds... yadda, yadda." She knocked back the rest of her coffee before continuing. "To give you a bigger picture. I have been on this case since they found your sister's DNA in the car in New York State. I have been working tirelessly on tracking her killers down. I am one hundred per cent team Garrick. I'm hoping that I don't need to persuade you to cooperate."

"You're doing a good job at persuading me." Garrick managed a small grin despite the dark thoughts swarming through his head. "You must have a theory on the identity of the others?"

Rivera shrugged. "I've been working with DCI Kane in London over this. We've hit a wall. What about you?"

Garrick used the time to fasten his shirt cuffs to marshal his thoughts. An idea had been percolating his mind for some while.

"John Howard. He's still alive."

Rivera tossed the coffee cup into a trashcan as if she were slam-dunking it. "He was burned alive in front of you."

Garrick recalled the snowy Wye street and the intense flames from John Howard's bookshop.

"I never actually saw that. I was unconscious."

"A body was found. DNA evidence confirmed it."

"I think we know the club is a little more advanced than most killers."

Rivera tried to think of an objection, but nothing came to her.

"I just think that's a little far-fetched."

"Killing somebody just because they have the same name as me. Luring me over here for a final kill... I mean, you really must redefine what is normal when it comes to these people."

Rivera glanced at her watch.

"Sorry, but speculation isn't helping. Right now, they think Grant killed you as planned. There is no cell reception at the ranch, so they don't know any different. But at some point suspicions will be raised, and they are going to have to come looking for answers. And we both know they're not dumb enough to drive out and take a peek for themselves. We can contain them in Flora. Once they get out, they can disappear. They're good at doing that."

"So we're going back into town?"

Rivera smiled. "I take it that's tacit approval, Risks 'n' all?"

There was no doubt in Garrick's mind that he was going to push this thing the rest of the way, no matter at what cost...

A chill ran through him as the events of the last couple of hours finally sank in. He could have died. He willingly walked into what he thought was the last confrontation. Thoughts of hatred and vengeance had clouded his judgement when he should have been thinking about Wendy and their unborn child. He felt a surge of guilt that they hadn't factored into his thinking. Perhaps Grant was correct, to a degree at least. They had warped him. Moulded him into something he wasn't.

"What about Molly and the others?"

"Ah. Well, they are problematic." Garrick made a gesture for her to continue. "They're suspects. I couldn't have them blunder into danger on one hand, or if they are in on it, I couldn't risk them telling everybody you're alive."

"What have you done with them?"

"Scott was arrested when a traffic stop found drugs in their vehicle."

"You planted drugs?"

Rivera feigned offense. "I would never do such a thing. But if it turns out they were there before he hired the vehicle, then I guess he's in the clear. It was enough to prevent Molly Meyers from interfering with you running away from the law. She's currently trying to play catch up."

"Why did you let me go? Apart from the fact I slipped under your radar?" he added smugly.

"Because you have form on this, David. The whole sorry affair was cracked open by you, even when people wouldn't listen. Even when your own people suspected you. You never gave in. And your instincts are impeccable."

Garrick nodded. "I suppose you've persuaded me. Let's go."

He took his Barbour from the chair somebody had slung it over. Rivera gestured to the door, and he took the lead. He didn't doubt Rivera's sincerity, but it bothered him. Particularly because she believed in his instincts.

And they were telling him that his hunch about John Howard being alive wasn't so fanciful after all...

1 5

GARRICK HAD IMAGINED thundering back into Flora in huge black Escalades with tinted windows. Jumping red lights with the full kick-ass authority the FBI commanded... at least in the movies. He hadn't expected sitting in the back of a battered Honda Civic, next to Rivera, while Hughes – the FBI agent who had served the coffee – drove. He couldn't help but notice they both wore bullet proof jackets and had SIG Sauer P226 automatic handguns tucked in their belt holsters. Rivera looped a small Bluetooth headset around her ear.

"We're on the move."

Garrick didn't ask how many people were on her team. He was sure her answer would be a simple 'enough.' Instead, his mind bobbed between the task at hand and a growing desire to contact Wendy. He only hoped DC Fanta Liu had acted on his email and checked up on her. He drifted back to when Rivera nudged him.

"Are you with us? I was just speaking to you."

"Sorry. I thought you were talking to..." he gestured to her earpiece. "We'll be there in forty minutes. We can reconnoitre and see who's on the move... but shout out any suspicions. We're flying blind."

Garrick glanced at the clock on the dash. They'd be in Flora a little after 9am.

"Molly Meyers is finally going to interview Sergeant Howard first thing, so they will be heading to the station."

"And who exactly are you watching?"

"There's only a small pipeline of communication between the UK and here. We know Grant was rushed into killing your namesake. As far as we can tell, the tank, the set-up, that was all purchased beforehand. The glass tank was purchased eight months ago from an aquarium in New Orleans. Grant had been working part time at the taxidermy place for two months. He had another job in an old people's home on the other side of town. We traced his movements close to Flora the night your sister went missing."

"So it's safe to assume he was there when she tried to escape."

"No hard evidence. You know how it is. But I'd make that bet."

Garrick allowed the slivers of new information on the timeline fall into place. He had spent months, over a year, dwelling on the case and absorbing information. Perhaps he had been too close to it all, and now was the time to take a mental step back and look at the bigger picture.

The image of Grant pursuing Emilie on that fateful night was difficult to shake. He was a big man, and she was petite.

He could imagine the terror driving her to cut off her fingers in order to free herself from the door.

Rivera voiced her thoughts, although this time her confidence was muted. "The obvious target here is Howard himself. He had full access to the case. Could hide or manipulate evidence. And Molly contacted him the moment she had confirmed your trip. He was the only one who knew you were coming."

"You tracked Grant here when my sister was killed. What about John Howard? He was here at the same time."

"That's when it gets hazy. He was a master at covering his tracks. We know he arrived in New York, then flew to Chicago. He probably drove from there. But if he stayed in Flora, it wasn't under that identity. He flew back home from Chicago."

Garrick had received an empty envelope, posted in New York, and sealed with his Sister's DNA. It was one of the first disturbing items he'd received in this twisted game. He'd taken it for granted that John Howard had mailed it. But this was the first time he'd heard the man had flown home from Chicago *after* Emilie's death, which meant another member of the cult must have mailed it to him. The same person they were hunting down in Flora.

Rivera continued. "We contacted every motel, hotel and Airbnb in the vicinity and were able to track down every one of their guests. One of whom was the Korean victim."

Garrick frowned as he recalled a name. "Ye-Jun Joh. A student who'd gone missing for two weeks." Her severed arm ended up at a crime scene back on his home turf. It had been shipped over and found by his old detective sergeant, Eric Wilson. That had resulted in his being killed by the Murder Club to hide their tracks.

Rivera nodded. "Which matched the DNA found in the car that contained your sister's."

Garrick gave her a curious look. That was news to him. Because he had been a suspect in a case led by the MET's DCI Kane, he'd only had limited access to information.

"Wait, so Ye-Jun was in the same car that crossed the State Line?"

"And made this a Federal investigation," Rivera nodded. "Whether she had been dismembered by then, we don't know."

"But she was staying in Flora, while being reported missing?"

"No, an Airbnb in Clay City, a few miles to the east. Or rather, she'd booked the premises before she went missing. We don't know how long she stayed."

"And what would bring a young Korean student all the way out here? No offense. But it's a bit of a dump."

Rivera shrugged. "Be offensive as you like. I don't live here. And we haven't been able to establish any connection between her and John Howard, either."

"What was she studying?"

"Medicine. A promising doctor, by all accounts. She was doing hours at a hospital in Chicago."

Something jangled in Garrick's mind, but before he could study what that was, Rivera brought the conversation back on point.

"And none of that helps us right now. Other than indicating the killers had local knowledge, and Sergeant Howard has never really left Illinois. And he was the only one who could have drugged you that night."

She'd made a convincing argument, but Garrick wasn't convinced. "It's very convenient. If I was being sceptical, then it almost sound as if *he's* being set up as a patsy. It's too perfect. Too circumstantial."

She threw him a sour look. "Maybe I was wrong about your instincts?"

"Do you think he torched the coroner's office?"

Rivera hesitated. "He was still at the crime scene at that point. But I said we think there were two people involved."

"And else? Your second suspect?"

"I was relying on you for that."

Garrick watched the farmland sweep past the window.

"Dugu. He's Korean–"

Rivera shook her head. "We checked for any connection between him and the victim. Nothing."

Something about this rankled Garrick. He'd had little information on the other victims, other than Emilie's fiancé, Sam McKinzie.

"What can you tell me about the car where the DNA was found?"

Rivera looked thoughtfully into space. "A Buick, registered to Morgan Keele. Another victim who was found beheaded at the ranch. His DNA was also found in your sister's rental, which was found at the scene a little battered up. It looked as if they skidded off the road close to the ranch."

How his sister had ended up at the ranch had been a mystery to Garrick. Once again, the fragments of information dropped into his mental picture of events, offering teasing glimpses at something just beyond his grasp. Like seeing images briefly form in the clouds before they dispersed.

"He was from Texas and serviced farm machinery. Why he was there..." Rivera shrugged.

"Airbnb..." Garrick muttered.

"You have them in the UK, don't you?"

Garrick threw her a bemused look. "From what I know of the area, Clay City is a one-horse town."

"They're lucky if they have a horse."

"So why would anybody advertise a room to rent, never mind want to go there in the first place?" He glanced at the time on the dash. "How far are we? Can we swing by? Show me the premises?"

"We don't have time for—"

"This is a perfect time."

Twenty minutes later they peeled off the interstate and past the two rival gas stations, the only ones in town. Main Street challenged Garrick's definition of the words, then they turned off and parked at the corner of a street. Agent Hughes cut the engine and pointed to a lone house a hundred yards away.

"That's the place."

"Who owns it?"

The two agents exchanged puzzled looks.

"We ran background checks. Nothing was flagged. Why is this relevant?"

"What's the situation at the coroner's office?"

Hughes spoke up. "Major damage. Front office was destroyed. Severe damage to the rear of the property, including heat damage to our victim. They've set up temporary admin at the hospital."

As he spoke, the front door opened, and a woman stepped out, half turning as she spoke to whoever was inside. She firmly closed the door and made for a pickup in the drive.

"Oh my God..." Rivera muttered.

Garrick nodded.

Agent Hughes frowned and pointed. "Is that... is that the receptionist from the coroner's office?"

"Good ol' Maureen," Garrick said, watching as she reversed from the drive, and turned onto Main Street.

"Follow her," Rivera said.

"She'll be heading to work. Not rocking the boat," Garrick said as Hughes started the engine and followed. With the wide-open spaces around him, he kept as much distance as possible between the vehicles.

"Okay, David, what's your angle?" Rivera looked at him intently.

"She must be hitting sixty and isn't exactly gonna wrestle a young woman to the ground."

"The person who torched the office walked in and out of the front door. I heard the key in the lock. The back door was already set up for breaking and entering... as if they wanted me there. The mere idea I'd destroy evidence fitted their bill. Her DNA would naturally be over everything. Eliminated instantly. And she knew where the report would be. In fact, she handed it to me rather than the Sergeant or Dugu. They were prompting me to head to Springfield."

"Evidence...? Anything tangible?"

"Of course not. They're not that stupid. My money is the house is in her partner's name." Garrick struggled to recall the conversation he'd overheard. "Cleveland. There would be no paper trail to her at all. Yet we can now connect dear Maureen to the arson and to Ye-Jun."

"Circumstantial. And this is a small town. A good defence attorney could connect anybody to anybody."

"Right. So check her internet traffic for last night. My money is on dear Maureen stuck at home caring for her partner and watching the pay-per-view of me getting my arse kicked."

As they entered Flora, Maureen pulled to the side of the road at a gas station. A teenager in a grey Chevy Malibu with a crumpled fender rolled towards her so the driver could talk. After a brief exchange, the Chevy pulled away, back towards Clay City.

"You still have agents at the ranch?"

"Watching it. Nothing overt."

"Tell them to expect that Chevy passing by."

Agent Hughes was already on the radio, relaying the Chevy's plates.

"None of the inner circle will go anywhere near the ranch unless they know things went well. I'm dead. And Grant is busy cleaning the crime scene. Pay a kid twenty bucks and she thinks they're ahead of the game. Get your guys to video him passing by." Garrick indicated the gas station. "They have cameras recording that exchange. It all adds up."

He could tell Rivera was impressed, but she did a great job of not showing it.

"And her accomplice?"

"Setting up the elaborate art deco crime scene was beyond her, physically at least. And Grant alone wouldn't have been able to do it. So somebody strong."

"Howard..."

Garrick bobbed his head doubtfully. He was still certain the Sergeant was a decoy.

Agent Hughes turned around in his seat so he could address them both directly. "So, what do we do with this?"

Rivera considered. "We need eyes on her. They're going to communicate soon." She turned to Garrick. "Check that you're dead." She tapped Hughes on the shoulder and raised her radio. "Get us within a block of the station. I'm going to call in whoever we've got spare to watch her. Go!"

Hughes ignored the speed limit as he drove them into the centre of town. Pulling up at the sidewalk corner next to a bank, Rivera and Garrick hopped out. The door was barely closed behind them before Hughes took off at speed. Rivera nudged Garrick toward the police station, and they set off at a brisk pace.

"I need your thoughts, David."

"I don't know. I'm making this up as I go. But I wouldn't waste resources on the Sarge."

"He'll be with Molly Meyers and her team now."

"In the police station? At least they'll be safe there." Several steps later he spoke his thoughts. "You investigated Molly's team. What's Kamila Ortega's history?"

"She studied television production in New York then pretty much stayed there, taking on an internship at NBC. Did a couple of years at Netflix before moving on to TBN, a religious network. Then became an independent producer. She's racked up dozens of parking violations, a few speeding tickets, but that's about all."

New York resonated in Garrick's mind. She was the first person Molly had contacted once she had the green light for the trip. She had access to everything. Their plans, location, their intentions.

Garrick stopped in his tracks. It took Rivera several steps before she noticed and stopped to turn to him.

"What?"

"Was everybody evacuated from the motel?"

"Of course. CSI still need a few days there."

"And everybody's possessions are still in their rooms?" Rivera nodded. "We need to look at Ortega's room."

Rivera looked him up and down. He still wore the same grubby clothes from the last three days. His chin was covered in short bristles and stained with grime. "You can't walk in looking like that."

DAVID GARRICK MARVELLED at the power of an FBI badge. Rivera had flashed it in a local clothing shop, had a quiet word with the proprietor, and the next thing he knew, Garrick had access to the store's cramped bathroom. It was beyond what he'd hoped to get back home. That would probably land him in an unwinnable argument that the toilet wasn't for customers.

Rivera had bought him a razor and deodorant from the store next door, and an Agent had been dispatched to drop off an FBI branded cap. Garrick wished the forces back home could look so effortlessly cool.

Arriving at the cordoned off motel, they received confirmation that Molly and the team had interviewed Sergeant Howard, who was apparently in a truculent mood. The local cops on motel duty didn't give Garrick a second glance as Rivera flashed her badge and they walked straight into Ortega's room, ignoring the do not disturb sign. It was next door to Garrick's and was a mirror image. The bed had been neatly made, and her oversized suitcase was against the wall. Her clothes neatly hung on the cheap clothing rail that served as a wardrobe. Peeking in the bathroom, revealed her toiletries neatly arranged.

Wearing blue Nitrile gloves, Rivera and Garrick opened the bedside drawers. There was a bible in one. Nothing in the other. With mounting frustration, Garrick patted down the hanging clothes, searching for anything concealed in her pockets.

"What exactly where you hoping to find?" Rivera asked as she lay the suitcase flat and unlocked it with a TSA access key.

"I don't know. A master plan…" Clothing pockets empty, Garrick turned around and eyed the bed. "A signed confession, maybe." He lifted the mattress. There was nothing underneath.

Rivera ran her fingers across the lining of the open suitcase just in case something was hidden there. It was clean.

"What if we're over thinking this?" she offered, closing the case. "What if it was just Grant and Maureen and everybody else is a red herring?"

"That would leave whoever was watching online."

Rivera nodded, returning the suitcase back to its original position. "And they could be the missing piece here. The ones with advanced notice you were coming."

Garrick pulled a face. "After all the effort, all the games, all the killings, why wouldn't they want to be here the moment they bring the hammer down on me?"

"Because they couldn't. Especially if they're supposed to be dead."

Garrick couldn't resist flashing a knowing look at her. "So now you think I'm not so paranoid after all?"

"That John Howard is still alive? I think it's pretty thin. But compared to the rest of my case, not improbable. And if he's hiding outside the country…"

"When will your digital team get results back?"

"CART is on it right now." she caught his puzzled look. "Computer Analysis Response Team."

"Is there anything you won't abbreviate?"

"You tell me, *DCI* Garrick."

Despite the tension knotted inside him, Garrick laughed, then became serious again. "We don't have long before they know what happened back at the ranch. And then they will do what they always do, scatter to the wind."

Rivera was about to reply when she suddenly cocked her head and stared into space. Only when she cupped a hand over her headset did Garrick realise she was listening intently. She slowly swung her gaze back to Garrick.

"CART said the IP addresses from the streamed audience were scrambled by a VPN." A virtual private network could pretend the user was anywhere in the world, making tracking them almost impossible. "But there were three people logged in. One of them must've had a glitch on their internet connection. It kept cutting out. And one of those times it reconnected before the VPN relaunched. The IP address was in England."

Garrick felt his blood run cold.

Rivera found it difficult to maintain eye contact as she continued. "In fact, it was in Kent."

1 ⁶

DETECTIVE CHIEF INSPECTOR *David Garrick died today. He was found with severe wounds at an undisclosed location in Illinois along with the body of another unidentified man. The FBI is treating the incident with caution as Detective Garrick was in American at the time as part of a BBC documentary team who were retracing the steps of his sister, Emilie Garrick, who died under similar circumstances.*

Garrick had read the lines several times. He had been assured it was a draft press release and would be refined before being issued, but now he was airborne he couldn't view the final statement.

The last four hours had been a maelstrom of activity. If there was no news of his death, he and Rivera agreed that the unidentified member of the group in the UK would vanish

without a trace. Strict protocol dictated that the UK authorities should be notified immediately, but as they did not know
who was leaking information on Garrick's movements,
nobody could be trusted.

Therefore, David Garrick had to die.

Agent Rivera had put across a valiant argument to her
superiors, which now resulted in them both on a chartered
private jet that had met them at the small Flora Municipal
Airport and was now hurtling them across the Atlantic.
Garrick had never been in such luxury before, but he had no
time to enjoy any of it. He took the opportunity to charge his
phone from his seat's USB plug and reclined the seat back to
snatch some sleep. But sleep refused to come.

The press release would be out by the time they landed.
In the US, Molly Meyers had been told the moment they had
taken off. Garrick felt a twinge of guilt about the angst she
must be going through, but he knew her well enough that she
would now be re-editing her documentary into focusing on
his death. In the depths of her grief, she probably thought
she had an award-winning hit on her hand. She was going to
be really pissed off to find out he was alive.

But his sympathies lay with his team. It was essential they
didn't know the truth. Rivera hadn't wanted Wendy to know
either, but Garrick had threatened to ruin the entire plan if
she wasn't notified. He'd wanted to send DC Fanta Liu, but
Rivera argued she was too much of a security liability.
Instead, they agreed to notify DCI Oliver Kane – and only
him – not the rest of his team. He was to discreetly contact
Wendy and take her to a place of safety.

Snatching twenty minutes here and there, Garrick kept
waking as the bizarre reality twisted its knife into him. He had

gone from a felon on the run to a dead man in the space of half a day. He could deal with that. What he had trouble dealing with was John Howard still being alive. It was hard to give credence to, even if it was his own theory. Garrick thrived on evidence. Even sporadic fragments of fact always helped consolidate a theory.

John Howard was believed to have burned to death in his home in Wye, Kent. Garrick had been there, although incapacitated at the end of their struggle. A body was found and identified.

However, Garrick had discovered that John Howard was at the head of the malignant Murder Club. A society, or cult as Rivera preferred to call it, that had recruits from all walks of life. Including the police. It wasn't beyond reason that the evidence was manipulated. Heck, Garrick himself was currently dead, so how far-fetched was it, really?

Work it through, Garrick told himself as he increased the blast of cold air from the vent above his seat. He was feeling hot and bothered. If John Howard was alive, then leaving the country posed a risk, although a man of his nature probably had multiple passports. Staying in the UK was only risky if the authorities thought he was dead. Which meant he could have been around Garrick at any point. Watching. Calculating...

But he was too high-profile a person to be able to get close to the investigation or to Molly Meyers. That indicated he had a henchman, a right-hand man to pull the strings. Three people had been watching, according to the FBI's digital team. He guessed that was Maureen, Howard, and the mystery man...

Garrick tossed and turned on the soft leather seat. He put his seat up and turned to Rivera to complain, but she was fast asleep with headphones on. Sleep would not come for him – *no rest for the dead*, he thought bitterly.

Instead, he took the iPad Agent Rivera had given him and started combing through the case notes on his sister's death. He had absorbed every morsel he'd been given, most of them in a series of phone calls with Sergeant Howard at the beginning of the case...

Garrick winced. Two Howards. Two Garricks... his nemesis really was trying to wrong-foot him at every turn. Garrick had never believed in coincidences. That had been the foundation of his career. Now he was being forced to challenge even that concept.

The file gave more details on Sam McKinzie's death, including photographs of the crime scene. Garrick was able to look at them with detachment. After all, he'd never met the man. He and his sister had been estranged since their parent's death. So much so, they had only established communication shortly before her murder.

McKinzie had been tortured with deliberate malice. Small acts of nerve damage and pain inducing incisions designed to prolong agony. His skin had been cut off with precision, a hallmark of John Howard who had used human skin to create book jackets and lamp shades which he sold on various dark web marketplaces.

Morgan Keele was the victim he hadn't heard about until recently. There were blood drops found in Emilie's car, but he had clearly been dismembered in the ranch. Had he reached to car to escape, then been dragged back? Without witnesses, the truth could only be speculated.

Ye-Jun Joh, the medical student, was more of a mystery. It appeared she'd been lured to Clay City, then to the ranch. Back in Chicago, she'd told friends she was going away from the weekend, but the Airbnb booking had been for two weeks. Like Emilie, Ye-Jun's body had never been located. Only a few specks of blood at the ranch and in the abandoned car that had crossed the State Line indicated she had been a victim. Her severed arm was later shipped to the UK to be part of a twisted hunt that had resulted in Garrick's old DI murdered and Molly Meyer's kidnap.

And that left his sister as the other known victim. Like Ye-Jun, only traces of her blood were found in the silo where Garrick had faced Philip E. Grant. Her fingers, still wedged in the metal door from where she'd been forced to cut them off to make her escape... and blood in the car.

Garrick frowned. He flicked back and forth through the file to find information on the car itself. It had been found abandoned in a ditch in New York State. Emilie's blood had been found in the back of the vehicle, indicating she had been held there. But reading through the forensic notes, Garrick saw the front of the car had been scrubbed clean of prints.

If both Emilie and Ye-Jun had been passengers, then the killer was taking a tremendous risk transporting them both. Unless...

Garrick silently berated himself for twisting the evidence laid before him. He was trying to find angles that weren't there. Couldn't be there.

Yet...

The working theory fit that his sister had been chased from the hangar and slid the door closed, trapping her fingers, and putting her in the thankless position of self-mutilation or certain death. She was escaping. Just how far had she gone? Had she and Ye-Jun escaped together? Had they been fleeing before the car ran out of gas, forcing them on foot – and their inevitable capture in the middle of nowhere? Of course, Ye-Jun's blood could have been in the car before his sister had taken it. But the Murder Club didn't do things randomly. They were thoughtful and calculating, no matter how twisted their actions. They collectively saw each kill, each tease to the authorities, as art. Sending Ye-Jun's arm as part of a deadly game had some deeper meaning nobody had looked into. Was it a simple statement of what happened to those who tried to defy the cult? But wouldn't mailing a limb from his sister be more impactful?

Garrick turned the iPad off. The screen's brightness was giving him a headache, and he was staring down a rabbit hole that wasn't helping his current predicament.

He tossed the tablet on the seat next to him and settled back in his seat as he stared at the blanket of clouds below them. They'd arrive in the UK in four hours, and they had no functional plan. The CART team was working with Kane to pinpoint the IP address, but once on the ground it would be a team of three, with no backup or resources.

All Garrick wanted was for the nightmare to end and to hold Wendy and tell her he loved her. He wanted things to be straightforward and simple.

But the nagging thought that there was *something* amiss in the report wouldn't go away. His eyes were drawn back to the iPad's black screen, as if it was taunting him to switch it back on and, instead of peering down the rabbit hole, jump in.

Garrick sucked in a sharp breath and resisted the impulse. He was stronger than that.

Three minutes later, he scooped the iPad off the seat and turned it back on. He scrolled through to report on the presumed timeline... and jumped down the rabbit hole headfirst.

17

GARRICK WAS FINALLY asleep by the time the Learjet landed at Lydd-London Airport in Kent. The name baffled most people, as the airport was 70 miles and a two-hour drive away from the centre of London. DCI Oliver Kane was waiting for them in a black Range Rover. He'd worked for a year with Agent Rivera, but their contact had been limited to emails and the occasional Zoom calls, but he was obviously taken by her when they shook hands. Garrick rolled his eyes; now wasn't the time for the middle-aged detective to be acting like a smitten schoolboy.

Kane followed the satnav, weaving the vehicle through narrow country B-roads that would have trapped the bulky US automobiles Rivera was accustomed to.

"We traced the rogue IP address to a property in Tenter-den." Kane glanced at Garrick. "It's a rental."

"Is that where we're heading now?" Kane nodded. Garrick knew it was the correct decision, but he still felt sheepish. "I was hoping to see Wendy first..."

Kane's face flickered between annoyance and sudden sympathy. "She's fine, David. I saw her myself two hours ago. I have somebody watching your house. She's got everything she needs. This is a ticking clock. There is an armed response team en route."

Garrick twisted around so he could see Rivera. "It must be weird for you not to be armed to the teeth. And remember, you're an observer now. I can't make you an honorary detective."

She pulled a face, which made Garrick smile.

"About that," Kane said with uncharacteristic tact. "You're an observer too."

"What?"

"Well, officially, you're dead, which puts me in a grey area, and you know as well as I do, we can't have anything questioning the investigations legality."

"Are you trying to tell me the defence will use the fact a dead officer was on a raid to undermine our integrity?"

Kane looked chagrin as he nodded. From the back, Rivera scoffed.

"And you guys think American law is weird."

Kane shifted in his seat as he changed the conversation. "Agent Hughes called me an hour ago. Molly Meyers was stunned by the news of your death, but predictable as ever, if currently roving around town trying to get more footage at the ranch. They've had to block the crime scene off, even preventing local law enforcement from entering." Kane frowned, not quite following the information he was reciting. "He told me to tell you the kid in the truck did a drive-past and U-turned back into town. Does that make sense?"

Garrick and Rivera swapped a knowing look.

"Nice piece of implication, Maureen..." Garrick muttered under his breath.

Kane continued. "He said they have eyes on the coroner's secretary, who completed her shift as normal and headed straight home. As yet, nobody else is behaving any different."

"So far, so dead," Garrick said ominously. He hoped their streak of good fortune would stay with them.

THERE WAS no way of getting close to the premise in Tenterden. The picturesque town had twice the population as Flora and gave Agent Rivera the completely wrong perception of England, especially as this was her first visit. They parked the Range Rover to the north of the town and Kane indicated a footpath that ran through a field.

"That seems to be the best line of approach on foot." The grass in the field had been cut, so they could see the track disappear into a copse of trees that hid the cottage.

Garrick drummed his fingers on the dash. "How long before the response team arrives?"

Kane looked at his phone and shook his head. "Still at least thirty minutes out."

Garrick popped his seatbelt off and opened the door. Kane looked sharply at him.

"What are you doing?"

"I'm going to inspect."

"The hell you are!"

"Relax. I'm dead, remember." Garrick shut the door before Kane could say another word.

He hurried across the road and clambered over the wooden stye, hopping down into the field. The short grass was damp from recent rainfall, but he still had his hardy boots he'd bought to withstand Illinois' snows.

Despite the horrors of the last few days; despite the physical and mental punishment mete out to him; despite feigning his death, DCI David Garrick felt as if he was finally closing a dark chapter on his life. It was a journey that had taken him to foreign shores then right back where he'd started, but retribution was close.

By the time he reached the trees, Garrick was panting for breath, but pressed on a brisk pace. He glanced behind, noting that Kane hadn't followed him. Despite their many differences and rocky past, he respected Kane and trusted his judgement, but even so the anticipation of waiting and doing nothing was more than Garrick could bear. He needed answers.

The wooded area was overgrown with brambles snagging his jacket and scratching at his face. The trail bent sharply to the left, and the trees thinned out, revealing a rotting wooden fence running along the side of the road. On the other side was a white cottage, with vines creeping up the walls and a thick thatched roof. It looked like a quintessential slice of England, not the lair of a sadistic serial killer. He crouched and kept to the shadows and peered into the dark windows. There was no sign of movement inside.

The best thing for him to do was sit and wait for the team to arrive and force entry, although he didn't know what to expect. No movement... and there was no car in the driveway, although a dirty blue moped was propped against the wall.

Was this really the home of John Howard? Had he really survived and gone to ground just mere miles from under Garrick's nose? It fitted within his duplicitous nature, yet Garrick was struggling to accept his suspicions as a reality.

DCI Kane had been certain the IP address pointed here, and there were no other buildings within two-hundred yards. A happy accident had led them to this location, but the killers were not known to make such blunders. And that made Garrick wary. The last time he had followed a clue into an unknown house, he'd led DI Fanta Liu into a booby trap that had destroyed most of the building and almost killed them both.

Now a task force was ready to break down the doors, and with it the three leading investigators into the Murder Club...

Garrick almost toppled over from shock as that insight struck him.

He pulled out his mobile and dialled Kane's number. The phone was fully charged... but in the middle of the countryside he had no signal.

"Dammit!" he snarled to himself.

If he hurried, he should have enough time to make it back to the Range Rover before the team arrived. He stood, intending to go back... but morbid curiosity stopped him. If he was wrong, they could ruin their one chance to end everything. The one chance to reset his life.

Garrick turned back to the cottage and scrutinised it carefully. Nothing stirred. The sharp caw from a nearby tree made him look up. A midnight black crow was perched on a thinning branch. It cocked its head to study him. Then another bird fluttered onto the branch, then two more. Three. Within seconds, a murder of crows noisily sat in the tree, peering down at Garrick with judgement in their soulless black eyes.

That's how it felt to Garrick. The truth was too tightly wrapped in a ball of misdirection, malice, and lies.

He had to know the truth.

He had to go in.

And he had to go in alone.

1 8

GARRICK PRESSED further along the trail as it turned away from the cottage. When he was satisfied that he was out of sight from any occupant, he darted across the road, vaulted a low wooden fence, and was soon in a paddock next to the building. He checked his phone. There was still no signal. He was sure he had five minutes before the armed response team arrived.

Hopefully, it was enough time to prevent a massacre.

The paddock extended parallel to the cottage, with a thick eight-foot-high boundary hedge between them. Garrick padded to where he thought he was parallel to the backdoor and pushed some of the undergrowth aside so he could peer through. The garden was overgrown, nowhere near as well tended as the front. A picnic bench and wheelbarrow were half obscured by weeds, and a pair of green and grey wheelie-bins were pushed against the back wall.

With no time to be subtle, Garrick pulled the FBI cap down to protect his face and shouldered his way through the overgrown hedge. Sharp branches scratched the back of his hands and exposed chin, drawing fine rivulets of blood. The hedge proved to resilient, so Garrick pushed his weight forward. Wood snapped as he forced his way through. Then the resistance stopped – and Garrick fell face-first into the overgrown lawn on the other side.

He lay still in the damp grass, listening for any signs of movement from the house. All was still. He angled his head, searching for any security cameras. So far, so good.

He stood and made for the backdoor. It was double glazed and when he tried the handle it was locked. Breaking the glass would most certainly garner too much attention. He needed a subtle way in.

Several rusting garden tools were propped against the far fence. A shovel, rake, hoe, lawnmower, and a wide scythe-like blade on the end of a wooden handle. He'd seen something similar once before, a spar hook knife used in thatching. He took it and looked up at the roof.

As stealthily as possible, Garrick clambered onto the wheelie bins. That brought the lip of the thatched roof to shoulder height. Wedging the blade in his belt, his fingers dug into the thick dry reeds, and he hauled himself up. It was a surprisingly simple move. Pushing the tips of his toes into the roofing, he pulled the blade out and sliced it through the thatch.

The dried vegetation easily snapped. A few repeated slashes, and the rusting blade cut through the binding straps. In moments, a hole was forming through the thick covering, revealing the narrow wooden lattice beyond. Garrick was so focused on the task at hand that he flinched when a distant train whistle pierced the air. It was an unusual sound, so out of time, until he remembered Tenterden was home to Kent and East Sussex Railway, a private line that ran a steam train for tourists. He was amused, thinking how Agent Rivera would react to it. She probably thought everybody in the UK was living like Harry Potter.

He soon had the hole big enough to slip through. Just a few strategic breaks in the wooden frame underneath, and he was able to silently slip into the loft.

It was pitch black, and his eyes refused to adjust to the surroundings. Garrick crouched, his hand blindly resting on the rafters beneath his boots. He couldn't hear any movement below and was beginning to think the house was empty. The train whistle blew again in the distance, prompting Garrick to hurry. He gently laid the spar hook knife across two beams and fished his mobile from his pocket. He noticed he had a single bar of reception, although it probably wasn't enough to make a call. He activated the flashlight and swept it around the loft.

At first, he didn't know what to make of the dozens of green plastic five-litre petrol cans placed across the loft in a uniformed pattern. Only on a second glance did he notice the filler caps were connected by a series of wires. Garrick gently tapped the one closest to him. It was full of liquid. With a pounding heart, he cast the light across the wires – tracing them to the hatch where they disappeared into the house below.

They had the correct house. And it was wired to blow.

Garrick's heart was pounding as he was torn what to do next. As he panned the phone's flashlight across the space, counting thirty containers in all. He noticed the weak reception had delivered a text message. It was from Kane.

MOVING IN!

Garrick swore under his breath. How old was the message? He had no illusions that the moment the front door was hammered down, the loft would erupt into a hellish inferno. A chair suddenly scraped across the floor below, followed by a rapid series of thumps and hasty shuffling. There was an occupant – and something had startled them. An early warning to somebody approaching down the lane? That would mean he had a minute.

Maybe less.

Garrick snatched the hook and jumped onto the thin ceiling – praying that there was something soft below to cushion his fall.

The plasterboard yielded with an almighty crunch as Garrick dropped through. The entire panel was plucked away from the joists, bringing with it a faux-elegant four-armed ceiling light several feet away. A plume of dust enveloped him, stinging his eyes. The lighting fixture smashed onto a dining table, while Garrick landed feet-first on the padded arm of a florid tuxedo settee. His knees gave way, and he crumpled arse-first onto the cushions before bouncing off and crashing through a cheap wooden coffee table.

He coughed as he inhaled the plaster dust and forced his watering eyes open. Somebody was standing across the room, frozen in a state of shock. He couldn't tell if it was a man or woman and could barely choke out the words.

"POLICE!" a hacking cough racked his chest, and he could only wheeze out, "You're under arrest..." before he lost his voice.

The figure suddenly ran towards him. He was still reeling from the fall as he made a grab for them. A foot smashed into his face, sending him sprawling backwards. Through his blurring vision, he could just see his assailant retrieve a laptop from the wreckage of the coffee table and slide it into a satchel slung over their shoulder. Then they sprinted for the back door.

It took Garrick two attempts to stand, as his feet slipped on the floor debris. His target swung the door open and sprinted outside. Garrick's hand fell on the haft of the spar hook knife, and he gave chase. Only a fleeting glance behind revealed shadows moving in the front garden. The armed response team had arrived – and they didn't know he was in here.

With renewed vigour, Garrick increased his speed out into the back garden. He gulped for breath with each step, spitting the foul from his mouth and trying to hack up the dust from his lungs. His target was already at the rear hedge, slipping through a pre-cut incision. He saw a hand raise, clutching a small object.

Seconds later, the petrol containers in the loft detonated in unison. A bright orange fireball punched upwards, vaporising the thatch, and blasting the windows from their frames – while blazing petrol rained down into the rest of the cottage. The shockwave was a body-blow to Garrick, and he almost lost his footing. His arms windmilled to keep his balance – and momentum shoved him through the gap in the hedge, into the field beyond. He collapsed to his knackered knees, grazing them as his trousers tore.

Behind, a thick black plume of smoke rose from the cottage, and he could see flames licking the sky. He hoped the police team hadn't been caught in the blast, but with his quarry sprinting across the field, he couldn't afford to check. With a grunt of pain, and spitting out thick dusty mucus, Garrick gave chase.

He'd never considered himself a fit man, and he'd lost count of the times he'd chased a suspect – through streets, fields, across glass roofs, airfields, and boat decks – he wondered why he never learned from his mistakes and settled on a health regime. But this time it was different. As if an inner demon had ignited an insatiable thirst for revenge. The stinging pains across his body disappeared. The aches in his knees and chest subsided and his breaths became measured and even. He gripped the haft of the blade and pushed himself harder. He wasn't catching up with the villain, but he wasn't losing ground either.

Ahead, smoke rose from the field's boundary hedgerow. He wondered what else was on fire. Now the tears had eased from his eyes, he could see the figure ahead was wearing a black leather jacket, dark blue jeans, and white trainers. A green canvas satchel containing the laptop banged against their hip with every step. It wasn't John Howard; it was some-body younger and fitter. Believing the son-of-a-bitch was still alive was nothing more than a flight of fancy; but this fresh addition to the Murder Club roster was obviously somebody of influence. With one hand for leverage, they vaulted over a wooden farm gate and Garrick lost sight of them.

Valuable seconds ticked before he reached the gate. He didn't have the strength for such an agile vault, instead he ran into the gate full pelt – throwing himself bodily over the top. Inertia flung him over, and it was all he could do to grip the wood as he once again fell onto his backside; a muddy puddle cushioning his fall. Cold water seeped across his lets and groin, giving him enough of a startling kick to jump to his feet.

The figure was sprinting down a narrow road, with semi-detached houses to the right, the owners' cars parked on the road, and a wall of trees and shrubbery penning them in on the left. The end of the road was a wall of grey fog. Garrick's confusion was fleeting as the figure disappeared into it – and he heard the shrill whistle of a train.

DCI Garrick increased his pace, ignoring the painful stitch niggling his left side. He ran into the plume of steam, the warm vapours helping clear his chest, but obliterating his vision down to just a couple of yards.

The road ahead curved to the right, but also continued into the car park of the train station. A fork to the left was blocked by the white gate of a level crossing. A steam engine whistled from somewhere in the smoke, and Garrick saw a train of four antique carriages slowly pull away.

His prey had caught up with the last carriage and was climbing up the black mushroom-shaped buffer. Garrick did what he always did in such circumstances. He didn't stop to think of the consequences of his actions.

With agility that surprised him, he vaulted the level crossing gate and raced onto the track, stepping on the sleepers between the rail, just about keeping up with the accelerating train. He slipped the hook into his belt and grabbed the nearest of the two buffers with both hands – just as he lost his footing. His legs gave out, and he was suddenly being dragged behind the train. The whistle merrily tooted again as Garrick clung on, the train speeding up with each passing second.

He saw the felon clamber onto the roof of the carriage without looking down, oblivious to Garrick's predicament. The sleepers bashed his boots as he rolled over them. Any faster and he risked shattering the bones in his feet. He knew he should let go and the train will be stopped at the next station – but that risked the mysterious person making their escape between now and then.

Powered by stubbornness, Garrick strained every muscle in his body, pulling himself up onto the metal buffer. With a grunt of pain and effort, he swung his legs up, hooking them across the metal buffer opposite. Slung between the two wasn't the ideal position, but at least he was no longer being dragged along the sleepers.

An access ladder had thoughtfully been screwed into the carriage's wooden rear. With extreme care, Garrick reached up for a rung. His cold, sweaty fingers gripped tightly – and he arched upwards, grabbing on with both hands. He was surprised he had the strength to pull himself up, but three rungs up, he was able to snag his foot on the bottom rung and climb up onto the roof.

Only when his head cleared the top of the train did he appreciate the speed they were now travelling at. The stiff wind slapped his face and the trees along the track were sweeping past in a blur. He estimated they were doing thirty or forty miles per hour, but it was impossible to tell. The fresh breeze now blew the smoke from the engine up and away from him, so he had a clear view over the roofs of the four carriages. The killer was already on top of the second carriage, slowly moving forward, their body bent in the wind.

Garrick's hand slipped on the smooth roof as he tried to pull himself up. He slid the spar hook from his belt and hacked the blade into the top of the old wooden carriage. It bit into the wood, anchoring him as he clambered up. Keeping his weight pushing into the wind, Garrick stood on trembling legs. He considered he possessed a good sense of balance, but with the constant breeze and the roof curving away either side of him, he knew acutely that a fall would be fatal. Clutching the blade, he powered forward, thankful his target still hadn't looked back.

The train swayed on the old track, forcing him to take small steps. The track languidly curved ahead, forcing him to check his balance – and to duck more than once as trees on their side whipped by. Garrick reached the gap to the next carriage. It was only a yard apart, but from the top of a moving, swaying coach it could have been much further. But there was no turning back. He braced himself and jumped. He landed with ease, which bolstered his confidence to hurry forward.

Ahead, the figure had reached the end of the carriage and faced the same dilemma Garrick just had. Beyond, the track made a tight left curve, which made the person hesitate. They glanced backwards – and froze in shock at the sight of a blade-wielding, dishevelled David Garrick lumbering towards them. They obviously recognised Garrick, but a thin veil of smoke drifted between them as the train took the curve, so Garrick couldn't see clearly. He rushed forward, capitalising on his quarry's hesitation.

The train's whistle blew again. Garrick suddenly dropped into a crouch as they took the bend and he felt himself inching to the curved side. He glanced from the drop to his right – to what lay ahead.

A bridge.

The whistle screamed as a stone bridge rushed towards them. At the last moment, his target turned to spot the wall of stone. Without thinking, they dropped into the gap between the carriages.

Garrick had nowhere to go.

He smashed the hook into the top of the carriage and threw himself as flat as possible. A millisecond later, the air pressure crushed him down against the roof. His Barbour scrapped the brickwork, and he felt the fabric shred. Smoke from the engine filled the tunnel, forcing him to hold his breath or inhale red-hot soot.

The train was moving so quickly that they popped through the tunnel in a cloud of steam. Garrick caught sight of a railways station as they shot through it with a merry toot of the whistle. He jumped to his feet and raced to the end of the carriage as a series of warehouses and fields opened around them.

Dropping to all-fours, he peered into the gap between the rocking carriages. There was no sign of his target. He wondered if they had fallen to their death, but then noticed the door leading into the third carriage was swinging back and forth.

Leaving common sense out of the equation, Garrick lowered himself between the carriages. There was no connecting platform, just the cold steel coupling mechanism below. If he slipped, he'd die.

The muscles in his arms quivered as he lowered himself, slipping his foot into the open doorway. He was under no illusion that his stamina was depleted to almost zero. With a grunt, he swung himself into the carriage.

His ankles throbbed as he landed in the narrow walkway that ran the length of the carriage to one side, with old-fashioned compartments separated by doors on the other. He could see these were filled with families and tourists. The killer could be hiding amongst them... but he needn't have worried. Sensing they too were at the end of the chase, the killer had reached the middle compartment and dragged one of the occupants out. It was a young girl, no more than twelve. The killer gripped her around the stomach with one hand, a kitchen knife poised over her throat with the other. The girl sobbed, her round brown eyes fixed on Garrick. Even in the throes of sheer terror, she was keeping it together better than most adults Garrick had met.

Garrick froze, renewing his grip on the blade in his hand. Now he could see the soot-stained face of the person he'd been pursuing. Confusion clashed with dawning recognition.

He knew the killer.

He just couldn't quite believe it.

1 [9]

THE DIRTY KNIFE blade pressed against the girl's throat. Even in the poor light, Garrick could see the dried crumbs and butter stains on the metal, confirming his suspicions that the assailant was improvising.

"Duncan?" Garrick could hardly bring himself to utter the name.

In his late thirties, Duncan Cook was a fit man. A member of the hiking group Garrick and Wendy had joined, he had quickly befriended Garrick on their walks. Constantly moaning about the state of the country and quibbling over everything, regardless of the political spectrum. His motor-mouth had quickly tired Garrick during the walks. He was opinionated, but he was certainly no killer. Garrick was sure of that.

"This wasn't supposed to happen," Duncan's voice cracked under the strain. His eyes bored into Garrick's. Pupils dilated, he was under the effects of drugs.

"Put the blade down. The girl is nothing to do with this. Bad decisions got you here. That doesn't mean you have to continue making them." As a sign of trust, he dropped the hook he was clutching.

"They said you were dead."

Garrick licked his soot-stained lips. His mouth was parched, and his voice sounded hoarse. He needed to keep Duncan talking until a solution to the stalemate presented itself.

"Who told you that?"

He saw Duncan tense. His eyes darting around to check that the girl's family in the carriage were still holding back. His eyes bored into Garrick with feral hostility.

Garrick changed tact. Logic and reason were not going to survive this confrontation.

"No one else needs to know this. Let the girl go and we can go back there and work things out." He jerked a thumb to the carriage behind.

Duncan's gaze flicked between Garrick and the door behind. A murmur from the terrified passengers rose as the carriage swayed as it took a curve. Duncan panicked and increased his grip, causing the girl to whimper. The swaying blade scored the faintest of red lines across the young flesh.

Garrick forced his most sympathetic voice. "You're not a killer, Duncan." He fought to remember what the man did for a job, but all he could recall was a library of eye wateringly dull conversations. "You're above this," he added desperately. "They're trying to use you, but they're not smart enough." Playing into Duncan's paranoia was the only course Garrick could think of.

"How would you know?"

Garrick shrugged. "Because I'm here with you. I bet they told you I was in America. Do you know how far away that is? I can't be in two places at once." The doubt shadowing Duncan's face gave Garrick some hope. He pressed on. "They're setting you up when you have done nothing." He prayed he was right about that. He still couldn't believe Duncan was anything other than a hapless idiot caught in the cult's web.

Duncan fractionally lowered the knife. Garrick nodded encouragingly.

"See? Nothing bad is going to happen."

One passenger, who was peering from a compartment behind Duncan, suddenly acted. The large, bad middle-aged man shouldered his compartment door open and thundered towards Duncan. Gripping the girl tighter, Duncan half turned as he reacted – but the have-a-go-hero was too fast. In the tight corridor, he wrapped his arms around Duncan and slammed him against the panoramic window. The girl screamed as she was pulled with them. Glass cracked under the weight and the continued pressure exerted by the big man across Duncan's throat. He was turning red, gasping for breath.

Garrick rushed forward as Duncan blindly stabbed the knife backwards. The blade thunked into soft belly flesh, and the big man gasped – suddenly loosening his grip as he clutched the stab wound him his abdomen.

Duncan tried to push himself away from the window. But it wasn't a solid wall he had slammed against, it was the door to the train carriage. As he moved, the screws holding the old lock pried from the wood – and the door swung open. Duncan and the girl toppled out–

Garrick was mid-leap. He grabbed the girl around the waist, twisting his body as he fell. He altered her trajectory and push her further down the carriage corridor. Duncan's torso lolled out of the carriage. Only Garrick's sudden weight on his legs prevented him from toppling to his death.

But Duncan was beyond logic. He thrust the knife at Garrick; the blade sliding into the meat of his left shoulder.

"Bastard!" yelled Garrick, as he squirmed in pain.

With his injured arm, he lunged for Duncan's throat. His fingertips dug into the soft flesh, and he could feel the thick muscles and veins beneath the skin. As the blade stabbed towards his face, Garrick used his other hand to grab Duncan's wrist and slam it hard against the doorframe. Now, only Garrick's own weight and the hand around Duncan's throat was all that was keeping them both from toppling out on the grassy embankment passing below at high speed.

Garrick repeatedly smashed Duncan's knife-hand against the door frame again with such brute force he heard the bones in Duncan's hand break and the blade fell from his grasp.

Snarling with fury, Duncan attempted to sit up. The fitness he'd gained from frequent rambling was paying off as he sat upright – and just in time as a signal post flashed passed, missing Duncan's head and Garrick's hands by inches. It smashed the swinging door, which broke off its hinges with a vicious crack of wood.

Duncan's strength ebbed, and he flopped backwards. Garrick quickly swapped his chokehold and wrapped his fingers around the man's t-shirt collar. His other hand anchored himself against the doorframe.

"Pull yourself up!" Garrick yelled. "I don't have the strength!"

Duncan didn't move. Perhaps he was as depleted as Garrick. He just stared.

"She said you were dead..." Duncan's words were almost lost in the wind blasting them.

"Who said?" Garrick shook him. "Who?" He shook Duncan with the last of his strength.

"You did so many bad things..." Duncan hissed. "They told me–"

They were suddenly plunged into darkness, and Garrick was splashed with water. The train's whistle howled – and they were suddenly back in daylight as they cleared the tunnel. Garrick saw his hands were bathed in blood. Then he saw Duncan had been decapitated by the tunnel wall.

Garrick threw himself backwards in sheer horror, propelling himself flat against a compartment door. As he was no longer weighing Duncan down, the corpse slid out of the speeding train.

20

2 *o*

GARRICK SHIVERED, despite the warm paper cup of tea in his hands. He sat alone in the carriage, while two confused police officers blocked the door. He'd glimpsed his reflection on his phone. He looked wild. His hands and face covered in black soot stains and blood.

The train had stopped short of Northiam Station, and Garrick had marshalled people to remain calm as they waited for the police to arrive. The sight of a wild, dirty man, covered in blood, did little to ease people's anxiety. The decapitated body blocking the passageway didn't help, either. Only the assurance from the grateful young girl's family to the other passengers lent any credence to his claims. Another passenger had come to the have-a-go-hero's aid and stemmed the bleeding from the stab wound in his shoulder. It was deep, but looked nastier than it was.

When the police arrived, he was immediately arrested. A situation made even more complicated when they discovered his warrant card, and then learnt that David Garrick was dead. Garrick's one call was to DCI Kane who, ironically, had assumed Garrick had entered the cottage and was dead for a second time.

The policewoman tasked with keeping an eye on him couldn't stop staring.

"So what's it like, being dead?"

Garrick gave the question some serious consideration. He appreciated the unusual predicament the officer was in.

"Not as peaceful as it's cracked up to be."

The officer's gaze danced between Garrick and the corpse. She must have thought it wiser not to say any more. The passengers and train crew, who had been oblivious to anything wrong, had been guided along the track to the station platform where a growing number of officers were assembling to deal with them. It was a good thirty-five minutes later when Garrick heard somebody enter the carriage from the engine side. He heard Kane's voice. Credentials were established, and the DCI finally poked his head around the carriage door. He blinked in surprise, half amused by Garrick's soot-stained face.

"Jesus, Garrick. You look like the hybrid love child between a racist and a serial killer."

"I'm fine. Thanks for asking." His upper left arm throbbed from the stab wound. The policewoman watching over him had competently cleaned the wound and apply basic sutures. Garrick refused any further medical attention. The fewer people who knew who he was alive, the better.

"Keeping a low profile, as we agreed. Good."

"The deceased is Duncan Cook–"

Kane indicated to the policewoman who had retreated to the end of the carriage. "She forwarded you statement and we're running ID."

"He was a member of the rambling club we joined."

Kane frowned. "I didn't have you down as the outdoors type."

"He's not a killer. He was already a member when we joined." He stared at Kane to see if he followed his point. Kane shook his head. "Which means he was recruited to get close to me." Kane let that sink in. "Rivera spoke about them as a cult. I thought she was just being *American,* but I think she's right. This has a *Charles Manson* vibe about it." Garrick finished his tea, his throat still parched. "Was anybody hurt at the cottage?"

"A couple of flash burns, but nothing too severe. It could have been a lot worse."

Garrick explained how he'd broken into the cottage and given chase to Duncan Cook.

"It seems the team has you to thank for their lack of fatalities. That could've been a tragedy. Cook was the name on the rental agreement. He'd been renting for three years. No previous criminal record. Was he a suggestible sort of person?"

"As far as I can remember he complained about everything. That's what seemed to entertain him."

"They confirmed tracing the IP address to that property."

"Can that be fixed?"

Kane hesitated. "I suppose it can. But he picked a cottage in the middle of nowhere. What were the chances it would have good internet? And I think we can take his guilt for granted." He indicated the body.

"'She said you were dead.' They were his last words."

"She? Are you sure?"

Garrick nodded slowly.

Kane gestured for Garrick to stand. "You need to clean up and get out of those clothes."

"Where? I can't go home. I can't go to the station."

"We'll book a room at a Premier Inn. I'll get somebody to run to Marks and Spencer and pick you something fresh up."

Garrick nodded. His legs swayed like jelly as he stood. We wondered if he'd have the strength to walk to the car.

Kane gripped his elbow to steady his balance as he stepped over the body.

"I want a list of everybody who was in this group. We're going to have to drill down on who he knows. It would have been useful to keep him alive, and not kill our only suspect."

DCI KANE'S organisational skills couldn't be faulted. On the drive to the budget hotel, Agent Rivera made notes who was in Garrick's hiking group and the last time he'd seen them. By the time they reached the Premier Inn, his room was ready. Kane was told to stay put and an officer would arrive with fresh clothing. He and Rivera were returning to the crime scenes.

The hot water and cheap shower gel provided by the hotel was soothing on his skin. Washing away blood and grime that turned the water black around his feet. His body was a map of scars and injuries. Gunshots, knife wounds, injuries sustained from explosions and fires. Garrick was surprised he was still in one piece. He trembled from the exertion he'd been through and thought if he closed his eyes now, he'd drop into a sleep that would last a week.

Thinking about Duncan and the rambling group led him straight back to Wendy. At least she didn't think he was dead, but he desperately wanted to talk to her. Kane had been firmly against that. He'd assigned an officer to watch over her, but paranoia was rife, and he didn't know who he could trust, even within the force.

After vigorously grating a layer of skin off towelling himself dry, Garrick wrapped a spare towel around him and collapsed on the bed. He was worried that they might have run into a dead end. The cottage was primed to destroy evidence rather than act as a deterrent or booby trap. And the sheer brutal forced employed indicated there was incriminating evidence there. Now it was all probably gone.

Duncan Cook had risked his life to flee, so he was aware of the implications. Their only hope lay on the laptop he'd taken with him. Garrick was sceptical that after such intricate plans, they'd leave a damning digital trail.

He was worried that this was as far as they would get. Thanks to him, the last vestiges of the Murder Club might get away with their deeds. He replayed events through his mind, searching for ways he could have dealt with the situation differently. After dozens of permutations, he still couldn't think of a way today didn't end in tragedy. It kept him on edge, depriving him of the sleep he so desperately needed.

A knock at the door made him sit bolt upright.

"Who is it?"

"Police," came a woman's voice.

Garrick crossed to the door. It must be the clothes he was waiting on. He reached for the handle... then hesitated. He peered through the door's peephole. There was a woman there, but she wasn't in uniform. She wore a black hoodie top, with the hood down, but was standing too close to the door with her head turned away to confirm her identity.

Had it come to this? He was so psychologically scarred that he was afraid of opening his own door?

Garrick huffed and quickly pulled the door open. The woman waiting beyond turned to look at him, her eyes widening–

Then she slapped him hard across the face.

"You bastard!" she snapped as she pushed her way into the room.

Dazed, Garrick touched his stinging cheek as a pair of plastic bags containing clothing were thrown at him. It took a moment for him to pull himself together.

"Fanta?"

DC Fanta Liu stood arms akimbo and glared at him.

"Why aren't you dead?"

"I feel I am," he said, closing the door and rubbing his cheek.

"Everybody had a melt down when they heard the news! And when they find out you lied about it, they're gonna kill you!"

Garrick scooped the bags from the floor. "They can join the line." Despite her indignation, Garrick couldn't stop the smile creeping across his face. "It's so good to see you Fanta."

Fanta pulled a face, on one hand agreeing and on the other not wanting to dismiss her anger just yet.

"Do you have any idea what you put us through?"

Garrick couldn't help himself. He laughed. "I just wasn't thinking. I'm so sorry."

Fanta couldn't maintain her scowl. It fluttered into an

embarrassed smile. "Well, now I have to give back all that money from the collection I started."

"Or we could split it. How much did you raise?"

Fanta swiftly switched the subject and indicated to the shopping bags. "I don't think it's appropriate standing in front of me wearing only a towel."

Garrick picked the bags up and went into the bathroom, closing the door behind him.

"Why are you here?" he called to Fanta as he took the clothes out. A pale blue shirt and tan chinos. Not exactly his style, but Fanta evidentially thought he needed to try a new colour pallet. She'd also bought a lightweight raincoat as his trusty Barbour was covered with congealed blood. She hadn't had the foresight to buy clean socks or underwear. He fished his old ones from the bath and hoped they didn't smell too bad.

"Kane called me. He said you needed someone you could trust. And I received the email you sent. Eventually. It was in my spam."

"Nobody else knows?"

"Well..." her hesitation alarmed him.

"Fanta?"

"Wendy knows." After an awkward pause, she added, "She was the one who told me."

Garrick rolled his eyes. Wendy just couldn't be tactful.

"She saw how hard I was taking it."

"You saw her?"

"Kane asked me to keep an eye on her. And since we've been through the wringer with these guys before, I suppose I know what I'm doing."

Of that, Garrick knew. Out of the entire team, DC Liu had suffered the most and proved herself invaluable time and again. He'd recommended her twice for accolades and promotion, but nothing had yet materialised. Which was a good thing, because that would mean losing her from his team.

"She said it was a ploy to weed the rats out."

"She should have said nothing," said Garrick sternly, although he was glad that she had. He stepped from the bathroom and indicated to his new attire.

Fanta nodded approvingly. "It's shaved decades off you."

"Thanks," Garrick said before he logged the veiled insult. That line of thought was suddenly closed off when another reared its head.

"Who's watching over Wendy now?"

Fanta gave him a look. "This isn't amateur hour, you know. There are *two* uniforms watching over them. So relax. They're two who've worked with you before. So they know how cranky you can get."

"Them?"

"Mmm?"

"You said they were looking over *them*."

Fanta nodded. "I thought it was best Wendy had company. Especially in her condition," she winked conspiratorially. "You kept that quiet."

"Her mother?"

"No. She called a friend. Sonia. She came over."

The knife wound in Garrick's shoulder suddenly twinged with a fiery pain.

2¹

THE THROATY GROWL from Fanta's pimped up exhaust pipe was embarrassing enough, with the sudden gun-shot pop as it peaked. And Garrick didn't think it was suitable for her little Ford Polo. She'd added mods to the engine, the latest being a blue LED lighting strip that traced the outline of the car and made it look as if she was driving on a cloud of blue light. It wasn't the sort of car that blended in, and he suspected that Fanta enjoyed the frequent traffic stops as officers were surprised to find a smartly dressed young Asian woman at the wheel. They were even more perturbed when she flashed her detective warrant card. But her wild driving was now an advantage as they sped towards Lenham, where Garrick lived with Wendy.

Garrick's thoughts waded through how Sonia and

Wendy had become friends. She had latched onto them during their hikes, but was often a taciturn figure who didn't engage in conversation and was often the butt of Larry's jokes. Larry was a big man who ran a print company he'd inherited from his Jamaican father. Garrick had wondered if the ribbing was because the two were in a relationship, but Wendy had laughed the idea off. Sonia was five-six and barely came to Larry's shoulder. They couldn't be more yin-and-yang. The fact he could remember more about Larry than Sonia spoke volumes. He couldn't even recall the woman's surname.

Nevertheless, Wendy seemed to apostle her and Sonia was often at their home or inserting herself into shopping trips. Garrick had always found her difficult to talk to, and more of an annoying feature in his life. He'd once tried to ask about her dating life, in the hope some luckless individual would be saddled with her, but he was certain she was single. With long wavy red hair, that was often uncombed and tied back, and heavily freckled skin, not that she was unattractive, she just made little an attempt to care for herself, which manifested in the occasional yellow-headed spot on her face. Despite this, he had been relieved Wendy had some company when he went to America.

Now he was regretting it.

"You're jumping to wild conclusions," Fanta said as she undertook a slow-moving car on the dual carriageway.

"I hope you're right about that."

He toyed with his phone, his thumb nervously skimming over the screen as he contemplated calling her or sending a message. He'd chosen to hold back. If Fanta was right, then he'd be worrying her for no reason. There had been a strict no-contact policy because they didn't know who was in on

Garrick's fake death, so she would be suspicious if he was the one who broke the rule.

Likewise, if Sonia was the *woman* Duncan Cook had referred to, then his call would destroy the ruse. That was if Wendy hadn't already told her. He hoped she'd had been cautious enough not to. Although he'd shielded her from the grim details of the Murder Club, she watched the news and occasionally wangled details from him.

"And there are two officers watching the house," Fanta reminded him.

Sonia wasn't a physically strong woman. When she walked down the street with was always with a degree of caution. Garrick had noticed she was never at ease around crowds. Which led his thoughts to Duncan Cook.

If he was right, and they were in a relationship, who had recruited whom? Neither was a gregarious character, and he couldn't recall them walking together. The rambles through the Kentish countryside often centred around a pub for lunch where they would all share a couple of wooden picnic benches and talk. It was the one thing Garrick had enjoyed about the group. It was the only time he didn't talk shop. The two club organisers, Mike and Stu, often talked about their wives and kids, with the group keenly waiting for the latest disaster report from a school incident, a spoiled birthday party, or home improvement disaster. It was never anything serious, just the lighter side of life going wrong, and Garrick found it was often hilarious. Mainly because it was happening to somebody else.

Studying the situation objectively, if either had deliberately inserted themselves into Garrick's life, falling in love with an unconnected party and bringing them fully into the fold of a highly secretive, murderous group was, to say the least, risky. But his job had also shown him that love makes people do the most desperate things.

"The house was rented by him," Fanta pointed out. "He was the one who ran..."

He knew she was trying to reassure him that Sonia wasn't a threat, but until he had confronted her himself, he remained unconvinced. His paranoia was cranked to the maximum. The only two people in the world he trusted were Wendy and DC Liu.

"So, when were you going to tell us about your daughter?"

Even feeling tense, Garrick threw her a half-smile.

"Daughter? I didn't say that detective."

"The nice thing is, if it's a boy or girl, you could name them after me!"

"Your dad named you after a fizzy drink!"

"Only because it was the only word he could read in English when he came over here, and the people at the birth certificate office were very militant."

"Could've been worse. You could be *Irn-Bru*. Or *Boddington*," Garrick grinned.

Fanta looked defiant. "My child is going to be called *Pepsi*."

"That is a weird family tradition. Naming your child so they're guaranteed to be beaten up in school."

"It builds character."

THEY'D BEEN SNARLED up in rush-hour traffic, so it was five in the afternoon by the time they reached Garrick's street. He told Fanta to park at the end, so that people didn't think the circus had come to town when they saw her vehicle.

Detective Constable Liu took the lead, relishing to

remind Garrick that, because of his questionable state of existence, she was in charge. On paper at least. Garrick was feeling irritated at being Schrödinger's Cop but went along with it.

He headed straight for the Ford Golf parked several doors away. It was an unmarked police pool car. Inside, a young plainclothes man sat playing a game his phone. He flinched when Fanta rapped on the window. He recognised her and quickly wound it down.

"Looking busy," she said with as much disapproval as she could muster.

The copper tossed his phone onto the passenger seat. "All's well, Ma'am."

Garrick wondered how much authority Fanta had applied to install such fear and respect to a man barely the same age as her.

"The premises are empty at the moment," he straightened up in his seat. "And officer Pendle is around the back. All's quiet there."

"Empty?" Said Garrick.

The cop frowned suspiciously when he looked at Garrick, but after a quick nod from Fanta he answered.

"The two occupants got into a car and drove off."

Garrick gripped the windowsill and loomed threateningly into the car. "Where to?"

The cop leaned back. "I... I don't know." Panic flashed across his face. "We were instructed to watch the house. Not follow anyone." He flinched when Garrick angrily thumped his fist on the roof. "The red head was driving."

"That's Sonia's car," Fanta said. "Put an alert out on her registration. Nobody is to approach them, just find out where they are."

"When did they leave?" Fanta asked as she typed an email to the rest of the team.

"An hour ago? They were both laughing. They looked fine."

Garrick paced back-and-forth, at a loss what to do next.

"It's going to be fine," Fanta said. "This is all bad optics." She didn't want to say more around the plainclothes officer. "I have to let DCI Kane in on this."

They had left the Premier Inn without notifying anybody. Kane had been adamant that Garrick needed to stay hidden until they had a handle on the situation. Garrick had agreed... in principle at least. That's exactly what he'd do in Kane's shoes. The only problem was it was all too personal, and Garrick was going to be damned if he was playing by a rule book his opponents had no respect for. Then an idea struck him.

"We can track her phone."

"That'll take time."

"No. She uses Find My Phone."

Since Molly Meyer's kidnapping, Garrick had insisted Wendy activate the service on her phone. It allowed authorised friends and family to access her GPS location. It was a very useful safety feature he had never used. He wanted Wendy to have her own privacy, so he never accessed it on principle. He was already walking back to Fanta's car as he opened the app.

Fanta instructed the copper to call her the moment anybody arrived at the house and caught Garrick up at her car, just as the phone map flashed up with a marker indicating Wendy's whereabouts.

Fanta sniggered. "Bluewater? They've gone shopping?" Bluewater was one of the largest enclosed shopping malls in the country. "Do you want to send a tactical team in to stop her maxing out your credit card?"

Garrick hesitated. She had a point. The stores were open late, there was a cinema, plenty of restaurants, and no reason to be suspicious. Although he longed to see her, it was the worst place for a reunion. And it still didn't erase the suspicions he harboured against Sonia.

Fanta picked up on his hesitation and smiled. "We could go in and you could make me a cuppa while we wait?"

He leaned on her car as he weighed up their options.

"Where does Sonia live?"

Fanta held up her hand. "We don't have a warrant to go breaking her door down."

"We don't have to actually break anything…"

Sonia lived on a new-build housing estate, close to Ebbsfleet International train station or the main Kent Police station where DCI had set up shop during his investigation over Garrick's involvement with the Murder Club.

The building company had applied their usual cut-and-paste design ethic that was making areas of the county indistinguishable from one another. Four-bedroom detached houses merged with smaller - but not necessarily any more affordable - terraced homes. Mingled between them were apartment buildings designed for busy executives who would commute into the vastly more expensive London, which was just two train stops away.

Fanta pulled up at outside the white-and-terracotta facade of a townhouse split into apartments.

"Number six, in there," she nodded towards the building.

It was six o'clock, and the skies were slowly drawing in for the night. Heavy black rain clouds pushed in with the threat of rain. Garrick studied the building as a large murmuration of starlings circled overhead. Their melodious calls amplified as they echoed through the concert canyons of the charmless estate. Garrick finally got out of the car and strode towards the apartment entrance.

"What're you doing?"

Fanta hurried after him and saw what had triggered Garrick's actions. A light had come on in the apartment entrance as somebody was preparing to leave. Garrick had timed his arrival just as the door opened from the inside. A man stepped out and saw Garrick miming his hand over the access keypad. Garrick beamed thankfully at him and held the door open.

"Oops, after you." Garrick gestured for the man to leave.

"Wait up, *dad*," Fanta called as she caught up, passing the man who was already listening to the music on his phone as he walked away.

Garrick held the door open for her. "Dad?"

Fanta shrugged and headed for a flight of stairs. Apartment six was on the next floor. The door was dark blue, just like the other three on the landing. The functional dark carpet still smelled new.

"I wonder how long she's lived here?"

Fanta glanced at an email on her phone. "Ten months, according to her tenancy agreement."

Garrick was impressed. Fanta shrugged.

"Chib is working the office hard. They still think you're dead. They've been running background on anybody who has crossed your path and annoyed you."

Garrick pressed the apartment doorbell. "In that case, we're going to need a library extension to the office."

Fanta indicated the door. "Are you expecting somebody to be home?"

"No. I was just checking there was nobody there. Otherwise this would be rude–"

With all his weight, he kicked the door lock. The blue door shuddered but held. Embarrassed, he tried again. This time the wood cracked, and it gave way.

"You can't do that!"

"I'm dead. I can do anything."

He entered the apartment. Fanta looked nervously around to see if anyone from the other apartments had heard anything. Nothing moved. So she quickly followed him inside.

"Well, this is certainly minimalist," Garrick said as she joined him in the living room.

It was completely empty. The walls were white and clean and there wasn't a stick of furniture. Poking their head in the bedroom and kitchen revealed the same Spartan conditions.

"Did she ever move in?" Fanta said as she tried the living room light switch. There was no power.

Garrick was crouching on his hands and knees, running his hand across the indentations in the short beige carpet.

"At some point. The question is, when did she move out? Must be recently if she's still registered as the tenant."

"And where too?" She caught Garrick's gaze and guessed his answer. "That's just speculation." She gestured to the room. "This isn't evidence. If anything, it's a lack of evidence."

Garrick inhaled deeply. Fanta had a point. That didn't mean he had to accept her interpretation of the facts. With his knees cracking, he clambered to his feet.

"Hungry?" Fanta nodded. "Come on. I'm going to treat you to dinner."

Fanta's brow furrowed. "Are you feeling OK?"

"I don't remember the last time I ate." He headed for the door and circled a finger around the broken lock fragments on the floor. "And keep an ear out for when this mess is reported."

Once Fanta was out, he closed the door as best he could.

"I know a little place we can eat at around the corner."

2²

"Bluewater?" Fanta shook her head as they pulled into one of the many spacious car parks.

Garrick was driving and enjoying every twitch Fanta made when he couldn't quite make the gear changes and was rewarded with a crunch. "You really need to get this gearbox looked at."

"After your driving, I'll have to do that now. You've knackered the gears."

Garrick parked. They walked towards the nearest entrance that lay over a small bridge, where a few geese lazily paddled even as it began to rain. The small entry plaza was home to a motorcycle pop-up display. A pair of Kawasaki motorbikes were being taken off dynamic display stands as a crew dismantled them. It was dark now, and the floodlights from the shopping mall lit up the white chalk cliffs behind them. The building's huge triangular shaped floor plan had been carved into a bowl scooped from the landscape.

"Just for the record, this is a bad idea."

Garrick gave a noncommittal grunt as he checked the map on his phone. He indicated to the right.

"According to this, she's over there and stationary."

They entered a space with restaurants on either side and an avenue leading further into the mall. Even at this late hour, it was busy with families and groups of teenagers looking for somewhere warm to hang out. Walking past a Waterstones bookshop to the left and an odd selection of a barber, a confectionary shop, and Ritual cosmetics, they entered the main concourse from the middle. It stretched left and right, where it turned sharply away forming another pair of wide avenues filled with shops over two levels. Escalators, busy with shoppers clutching sales bags, joined the two.

"Most of the restaurants are this way," Garrick pointed out as they neared Marks and Spencer, that dominated the corner. The boulevard branched off to the left. Midway down a knot of restaurants branched off to a right-hand side passage near the cinema. Garrick stopped, suddenly uncertain.

Fanta was several steps ahead before she noticed. "What's wrong?"

"I'm thinking you might be right."

"Wow. Well, that's never stopped you before."

Fanta smiled playfully, but all Garrick could see was the scar on her forehead. It had healed well, but it was a permanent reminder of how things went wrong in the past when Garrick pursued his hunches. They had triggered a booby trap, which had almost killed them. Garrick's body was a roadmap of scars. A constant canvas of poor decisions and the aftermath of taking risks before thinking.

Yet again it felt as if he was reliving the same decisive moment.

Fanta was following him with blind trust. Break protocols with an eye for the greater good. Ahead was his pregnant girl-friend... partner... he was still fumbling over the definition. But what was not in question was that it was the woman he loved, carrying their unborn child. It was his greatest weakness, and he had zero doubt any member of the murderous cult he was pursuing would exploit it.

And if he was wrong about Sonia, then the damage his suspicions would cause risked Wendy losing a friend she had become close to. It even risked damaging their relationship. She was the most understanding woman he had ever met, but he was certain there were limits to such tolerance. This was a belief that fed into deeper conflict. He could never understand why she had stayed with him.

They'd stumble across one another on a dating site which had proved useless until that point. Their first date had been an utter disaster, yet something had made him reach out to her again and, to his surprise, she had thought they should give it another go.

Despite him going viral on social media when he recklessly chased a suspect; despite his constant injuries; and despite the kidnapping of people close to him, he and Wendy had moved in together and were having a child. To Garrick, that was the most unbelievable part of this whole thing.

"David?" Fanta nudged him out of his reverie. She looked concerned, keeping her voice low. She seldom used his given name but didn't want to say anything that would broadcast they were police detectives. "What's wrong?"

Garrick shook his head, unable to vocalise the thoughts clashing in his mind. His temples throbbed, hinting at a migraine yet to come.

"I don't know. Something feels off..."

Fanta gave a sardonic smile. "Everything about this is off. That's the normal default for things going wrong."

Garrick moved over to the window of a jewellery shop on the corner and pretended to peruse their selection of eye-wateringly expensive wrist watches. Fanta joined him, conscious that he was using the reflections to help keep an eye on what was happening around them.

"It feels like a set-up," he said bluntly.

"To what end? It's a pretty public place for an ambush."

"Exactly. The sort of newsworthy last stand type of desperation they're likely to do if they're cornered."

"They think you're dead."

"Do they? Won't they get suspicious that Grant hasn't reappeared? That he didn't post my death in glorious detail?" He paused, watching as Fanta absorbed his line of thinking. "If Sonia and Duncan are together in this, would she wonder why she hasn't heard from him?"

They had checked the local news on the drive. The fire at the cottage had yet to make any headlines. The media were more focused on the *incident* onboard the train. So far details hadn't leaked, and it was sufficiently far enough from Tenterden that it might not raise immediate suspicions, but it was all just a matter of time.

Fanta sighed. "You're painting us into a corner. This is all just assumptions and guesswork based on tenuous evidence."

Garrick placed the palm of his hand against the storefront glass to steady himself. Fanta glanced at him with concern.

"Are you feeling alright?"

Garrick searched for his words. Emotions swirled that were unfamiliar to him, but he finally anchored on to what was causing him so much stress.

"I feel like I'm about to lose everything."

Fanta awkwardly laid a hand on his back. She wasn't the most tactile person, so felt as uncomfortable as Garrick did.

"Look, you don't have to do anything," she said softly. "I can check up on her. She won't even see me." She handed Garrick her car keys. "Why don't you sit in the car?"

In the past, Garrick had felt as if he was becoming irrelevant. Knowing that his DC had made a good point, he felt increasingly redundant. He was grasping at straws. Combining ideas and fears without evidence. If this was one of his team on a case, he would have been furious. It was unprofessional, and yet here he was doing it himself. It was yet another sign that the Murder Club had got to him; stripped about everything he held dear. And that included his ability to be a good detective. Garrick hesitated before accepting the keys.

"Thanks," he said. "I think that's a good idea."

"Good. I'll find her and get back to you." She started to move before returning to Garrick with her hand outstretched. "It would be useful to know where she is."

Garrick's brow furrowed before he realised what she meant his phone. He unlocked it, called up Find My Phone, and passed it to her.

"See you in the car."

Fanta hurried away. Once again, Garrick hesitated. He felt compelled to go after her, but knew he'd be in the way. With heavy feet, he turned around and headed for the car park.

He reached the branching corridor that led past the bookshop and towards the car, when he got the distinct impression that he was being followed. At first, it was a sixth sense honed from countless hours watching his back when he was a regular copper on the beat. It was a skill he, and others like him, had grown to trust.

He passed a shopping mall security guard. The man was in uniform, but Garrick doubted he possessed skills any more advanced than shooing teenagers away. He made the most of the reflections in the shop windows as he turned into the corridor.

A figure in a black hoodie top made the turn seconds later. The reflections were not enough to make out details, and Garrick didn't want to stare straight at them and blow the gaff, at least not yet.

Or was he being paranoid? Other people made the turn too. It was still quite busy. He berated himself for handing Fanta his phone. He felt oddly unarmed without it, and after the wild day he'd had, he wasn't feeling physically in shape to make a run for it or face his phantom pursuer.

At the last moment, he took a right into the ground floor of the bookshop. He tried to move casually and headed for the directory on the wall, outlining the various sections within the shop. He pretended to look, then headed up the staircase.

Now on the first floor, he made for the local history section. The shelves were too close together to give him a clear line of sight behind, so he wasn't sure if he was still being followed. If he had been at all.

He made a pretence to look at the books before heading out of the closest door. He stepped on another wide avenue, like the one below, lined with an assortment of shops. Aside from the Starbucks opposite, clothing shops dominated most of the retail space. Garrick made a beeline for the Barbour shop and pretended to admire the jackets in the window as he scanned the reflections behind him. It wasn't ideal. The shifting forms of shoppers gnawed his paranoia.

Was Sonia following him, or was she with Wendy? If it wasn't her, who was this new entity... or was the wrath of his hallucinations returning at the height of stress? While he bore the delusional effects caused by a benign tumour pressing on his brain, the vivid auditory and visual phantoms that had been plaguing him had subsided.

But not completely vanished.

He closed his eyes and lent his forehead against the window, leaving a greasy patch on the glass. He breathed in deeply in through his nose and out from his mouth, regulating his anxiety.

I'm in control, he assured himself.

He didn't know how long he stayed like that. He opened his eyes and studied the reflections again.

There was a hoodie figure standing on the threshold of the bookshop. A woman.

And she was staring straight at him.

2³

SOMETHING IN GARRICK SNAPPED. A white rage manifested in his solar plexus and felt as if it surged along his spine before branching out down his arms and legs. Like a tsunami, it wiped aside his aching pains and fatigue. This was one game too far. One goading prompt to throw him over the edge. All this time he had been resisting playing their game, but what if *that* was their game all along?

He would not take it anymore. He was going to throw caution to the wind and play their game.

He quickly spun around and charged as fast as he could towards the hoodie wearing woman. She had already anticipated his move and had turned to the side, obscuring her face, as she ran towards the down escalators. In the heat of his rage, Garrick shouldered aside a guy in a t-shirt, who went sprawling across the floor – his shopping bags sliding every which way. Ignoring the barrage of swearing, Garrick pressed on as the woman reached the top of the escalator. The steps down were clogged with shoppers, making it almost impossible to push through.

He had her now!

A solid force suddenly struck him from the side and Garrick was suddenly on the floor with a weight crushing the breath out of him. He flailed his elbow, connecting with the side of his attacker's face.

"Calm down, mate!" came a voice close to his ear, carrying the smell of cheese and onion crisps with it, as the weight shifted to pin him down.

Garrick caught a flash of a crisp white uniform and realised it was the store security guard he'd judged as too useless to do anything. The one advantage Garrick hadn't factored in was the man's excessive size. The sheer pressure was pushing his arm to the ground as the guard tried to pin him.

"I'm the police!" Garrick wheezed.

"Sure," came the unconvinced replied. "Then take it easy–"

Garrick was in no mood to explain himself. He wasn't a dirty fighter, but now he needed to abandon his principles. His knee lashed down, plating firmly in the man's groin. At the same time, he butted him. He wasn't aiming for his face, but the soft throat that was inches from his. The combined blows caused the security guard to buckle to the side. Garrick rolled to his feet as the man crumpled into a world of private pain.

In a few strides, he was at the escalator. He could see the woman's head near the bottom, looking in his direction. As soon as she spotted him, she turned away and shoved between the last few people between her and the ground floor. Garrick instinctively made for the gap between the up and down stairwells. Unlike what he'd been conditioned in movies, there was no slope he could slide down like an action hero. It was a drop to the floor below.

Garrick kicked wildly as he fell. Immediately beneath, in the lee of the escalators was a bagel stand. He crashed through the plywood roof and onto the wood display case below. The lines of freshly cooked bagels did little to cushion his fall, but the impact knocked him sideways into a pair of teenage staff who did.

He scrambled through the wreckage, ignoring the swell of concerned voices around him, and saw the hoodie was already halfway down the corridor exiting to the car park, limbs pumping furiously in their bid to escape. Ignoring the pain shooting up his leg, Garrick gave chase.

They sprinted through the entrance lobby, past the lower Waterstones entrance and towards the doors leading out. His stalker was far head, and their lead was only increasing. The fall from the escalators had done something to Garrick's leg, and now a dull pain throbbed through it. But he was damned if he was going to quit this chase.

Even as that thought formed in his mind, the hoodie shouldered open the glass plated door and was outside. Garrick redoubled his efforts and reached the door before it had time to swing shut. He barrelled headlong into the plaza.

Night had rapidly descended, and the area was now lit by stylishly planted lights that played over the pond ahead – and the motorbike display that was in the process of dismantling for the evening. Like a series of snapshots, Garrick took in the prone salesman on the floor, clutching his stomach. His fingers were tinged with blood as he stemmed a wound. Garrick's quarry was on one of the motorcycles, the engine already howling as they twisted the throttle, a bloodied knife still in their hand. Rubber burned as the back wheel spun on the spot – then the bike sped up across the plaza and over the bridge – startled shoppers screamed as they darted aside to clear a path.

Garrick ran to the bleeding man's side, but his colleague was already there. He instinctively wanted to help, but his eyes were dragged back to the fleeing hoodie.

He forced his gaze back to the colleague. "Do you know first aid?"

The man, a pimply twenty-year old, nodded dumbly – then snapped out of his shock and pulled his jacket off to stem the wound.

"Good." He looked up and roared at the crowd assembling around him. "Call an ambulance!" He saw two people turn to their phones, while others stood and gawped. One woman was filming the grizzly scene. He patted this first aider on the shoulder. "Helps on the way. I'm the police. I'm going to need that bike."

He nodded to the other Kawasaki, then hurried towards it. Before anybody could stop him, Garrick was sitting on top and turning the engine over. He'd rode a motorbike in his university years, but not much since then. He just hoped the old adage that you never forget to ride a bike, also applied to motocross. He kicked the stand up and shot off towards the bridge at such a speed he lolled backwards, pulling the bike into a wheelie. Terrified, he thrust all his weight forward, the front wheel kissing the ground.

In the blink of an eye, he was over the bridge and in the car park. Ahead, the other rider had hit problems trying to leave the lot as a lorry had taken the wrong turn and was blocking the road. They planted a foot on the ground and slewed the bike sideways, cutting back across the carpark.

Garrick changed course, speeding to intercept the rider who hadn't yet seen him. Garrick was so focused on his target that he almost did not see a car reversing from its bay, rolling directly in his path. At the last second, he jinked the Kawasaki around it. The growl of his engine and the screech of the wheel made the hoodie look around. He saw a flash of the feminine face. It was definitely a woman. As soon as she spotted him, she hunkered low over the handlebars and sped down a narrow aisle of parked cars.

After losing the imitative, Garrick altered course to give chase. He briefly wondered which way the woman would go to escape from the lot, before he realised that she was aiming straight for the sliding glass doors leading into Marks and Spencer. At the last moment, she popped a wheelie, using the bike as a battering ram. The glass door didn't have time to part before shattering into a million fragments as she burst through it.

Garrick swore loudly as he followed into the store, at high-speed.

The lead bike's tyres screamed as they hit the polished white tiled floor. The Kawasaki was designed to be used to a range of surfaces, including slick muddy conditions, but the floor was more akin to ice. Until now, the woman had showed masterful control of the machine – but even she was out of her depth. She wrestled the front wheel side-to-side to keep her balance, braking as the bike slid sideways. A thick black line of rubber across the floor followed in its wake. She body slammed into a hulk of a man in a red lumberjack shirt. He flew into a rack of coats as she regained control and threaded her way through the men's clothing aisle.

Garrick had a little more luck. His wheels crunched across the broken glass as he rapidly slowed. He veered around a store clerk who was frozen in terror – his handlebar raking across a display of shirts, yanking them off the rail.

A cacophony of screams rose as the startled shoppers ahead of them realised what was happening. The woman picked her way through the displays at speed, kicking aside a middle-aged security guard who made a grab for her. As soon as she was clear of the outdoor clothing display, she spurred the bike forward towards the exit.

Desperately trying to recall his bike riding skills, Garrick raised himself a few centimetres from his seat and leaned forward as he twisted the throttle as he gave chase. The woman was now erratically weaving through stunned shoppers, each arcing path slowing her down just enough for Garrick to catch up. They reached the exit just as he gunned the throttle – his front tyre impacting into her rear wheel. The rider fought to keep her balance as she was shunted along. Garrick's hope that she'd fall off the bike was thwarted. Instead, she accelerated, the motion enabling her to regain her balance. In an instant, they were both hurtling down the busy shopping centre boulevard at high speed. It was irresponsible. Garrick knew the safety of the civilians around them was priority and he should shut the mall down and contain the suspect.

But an inner demon spurred him on. He instinctively knew this was the last roll of the dice when it came to the Murder Club. If they failed now, he half suspected they would disperse into the shadows for years, maybe decades, and he doubted that any investigation, no matter how

focused, would track them down. They either complete their
torment against him or disappear. A victory in either case.

Midway down the avenue, the woman drifted towards a
central escalator. Garrick's heart was in his mouth as she
suddenly leaned back and pulled the bike onto one wheel,
seconds before hitting the metal steps. The front wheel
crashed down, allowing her to power up the downward
moving escalator.

Mustering every childhood memory from his youthful
days in Liverpool when he had dominated the local streets on
his Raleigh Chopper, a bicycle with a high-back seat that was
the epitome for cool in the seventies, he clutched the handlebars tightly and stood up on the Kawasaki's pegs, ready to
pop a wheelie.

His childhood practise paid off. He was almost thrown
headfirst over the handlebars as he struck the moving staircase, but he throttled forward and upwards with grim determination. Each step jolting the bike and snatching his breath
– but then he was up onto the next level. Already the woman
was charging past Boots, a security guard inefficiently waving
her arms, hoping to slow her. Garrick's bike screamed as he
gave chase.

Once again, shoppers either fled aside in panic or were
frozen to the stop in astonishment, forcing the riders to
swerve aside. With laser-like focus, Garrick pushed his
motorbike for all it was worth. It would have been an even
race if the woman hadn't been forced to slam on her brakes to
avoid a knot of teenagers who were filming the chase on their
mobile phones.

Now Garrick was alongside – and time appeared to freeze.

It was Sonia. She glanced sidelong at him. It was the
briefest of looks, but it conveyed hatred and a malice he had

never experienced before. His first reaction was defensive; what had he done to deserve such ire? A split-second later it was replaced by rage.

Garrick leaned towards her. His bike responded, covering the six-inch gap between them in a second. His shoulder smacked against her head – but the clash was amplified by the speed they were going. Sonia suddenly wobbled and tried to roll to the opposite side, but she was too near the barrier in the centre of the boulevard. She bounced off it at thirty miles per hour. Garrick was already braking, skidding his bike sideways as the tyres struggled to keep a grip on the polished tiles as they left an arcing black streak of rubber.

Sonia desperately tried to counterbalance. Instead, she crashed to the floor. She was a small woman. The weight of the bike crushed her right leg, pinning her to the floor and dragging her along. Grey smoke fumes from the stressed engine clouded the details but left a trail of blood and petrol as she was dragged forward at speed–

Straight into the reenforced glass barrier that lined the upper corridor. It was designed to take the impact of a person, not a fast-moving lump of metal. The reinforced glass exploded as the stricken Kawasaki ploughed through it, dragging Sonia along for the ride.

Garrick just about stopped his bike before he crashed into the glass storefront. He was half-off the bike and running towards the barrier as he watched Sonia and the Kawasaki soared through the air. The bike rotated almost three-hundred-and-sixty degrees, separating Sonia from the machine. She was spinning like a rag doll as they both crashed to the level below, slamming into a wooden cart selling phone paraphernalia, and then on through another stall selling bubble tea. The flimsy carts were destroyed by the rampaging motorbike. Then it hit the stone steps of a central ornate staircase and came to a rest with the engine still screaming.

Garrick rushed towards the top of the same steps, his view blocked by the balcony, so he could not see where Sonia had ended up. He was several steps down when the scent of petrol hit his nostrils. The Kawasaki's engine screamed like a banshee. Then ignited.

Garrick recoiled from the blast of heat as an orange fire-ball punched towards the ceiling as the bike's petrol tank exploded with a bang that hurt his ears. Seconds later, the fire sprinkler system activated, emergency sirens blasting, as it rained inside the shopping centre.

2^4

EACH PEAK of the ECG machine felt like a needle in Garrick's temples. He leaned against the hospital room door jamb and stared hard at Sonia who lay in the bed, a metal armature holding her neck and head firmly in place. Another supported her mangled right arm. As a nurse checked her fluid levels, Garrick fantasied about replacing the saline with acid and watching the bitch burn from the inside out...

He took a deep breath and tossed the thought aside. He needed to be in control, and that was no easy feat at the moment. The one person with any useful information had been unconscious since the motorbike crash in the shopping centre, and the doctors were unsure about her prognostics. She'd suffered a head injury and there was no guarantee she

would even recover. Her vitals were low. It was a miracle she
was still alive at all.

The last moments in Bluewater ricocheted around
Garrick's head. Sonia's crashed motorbike had leaked fuel
and exploded, triggering the fire sprinklers. By the time
Garrick had descended the staircase, a pair of men were
dragging Sonia from the flames. She had been pinned down
by the bike and suffered burns on her legs. Her head had hit
the floor on impact, and without a helmet, her skull had frac-
tured. Garrick hadn't been able to get close before security
descended on him, pinning him to the floor as others tackled
the flames. It took some time for the arriving police to
untangle what had happened and establish Garrick's identity,
by which time Agent Adriana Rivera and DCI Kane had
arrived. What concerned Garrick initially was the disappear-
ance of DC Fanta Liu. Ordinarily she would have been one of
the first at the scene. The public had been evacuated from
the building, but Wendy wasn't amongst them. He and Kane
had spread out, checking and double-checking everybody's
face. Sonia's car was still in the car park, but Fanta's had gone.

Sonia had been carefully placed in an ambulance, and
Garrick had insisted on riding with her. Kane instructed
Rivera to accompany him. A move Garrick thought was done
to make sure he didn't beat a confession from the woman.

By the time they'd arrived at the Queen Elizabeth Hospital, Kane telephoned Garrick to report that the shopping
centre's surveillance recordings of the entire incident were
deleted. There was nothing of the chase. No images of Wendy
and Sonia meeting. Even the car park recording had disappeared. They had been deliberately purged. There was no
record of Wendy or Fanta leaving the site, and Fanta's phone
was off.

They had disappeared.

Police had been posted around Sonia's ward. Garrick had been taken to A&E to have the network of tiny glass cuts cleaned. The heat blast from the explosion had left the skin on his right cheeks tender and with a red hew as if he was suffering a mild rosacea. When he had returned to Sonia's ward, he'd found his long friend and colleague DC Harry Lord had been posted at the door. His hard glare at the woman in the bed had transformed to one of shock when he saw Garrick.

Garrick managed a weak grin, guessing where Lord's imagination was already taking him. "Relax, Harry, I'm not the undead."

Lord looked blankly between Sonia and Garrick, then finally found his voice.

"When this one was turned in, I thought she had all the traits of a botched heavy-handed arrest, but I thought, nah, can't be the Guv because Fanta already screwed twenty quid out of my for the funeral collection."

"Well, technically, I haven't even had a chance to arrest... wait, twenty pounds? That's all you put in my wake kitty?"

Lord shrugged and paced around the bed, still recovering from his shock and hiding behind a wall of bluster.

"That's all I had on me. And I was going out that night too. Really inconvenient. I missed the movie I was supposed to see. While you're faffing around going undercover."

"Doesn't get deeper than being dead."

The two men stared at Sonia, with only the regular tone from the ECG punctuating the silence.

"Chib's gonna be annoyed."

"Because I'm alive?"

Lord's head bobbed side-to-side. "Promotion opportuni-

ties are few and far between. And after all your recommenda-
tions..." The flicker of a smile gave away his satisfaction at
teasing his boss. "I'm not gonna be the one to tell her. Or
Wilkes."

"They'll live."

"Like you do, apparently."

Garrick solemnly shook his head. "Twenty bloody quid..."

After a few minutes of silent contemplation, the serious-
ness of the situation resurfaced.

"Still no word from Wendy or Fanta," Lord said. "CCTV at
Bluewater had been erased from an hour before you arrived.
The old tape backup wasn't on, either." He looked meaning-
fully at Garrick. "The security guard there is 'helping with
enquires'," he made air quotes with his fingers. He didn't
believe it was a coincidence.

Garrick nodded at Sonia. "Any link to her and Duncan
Cook?"

Lord looked puzzled for a moment. "Cook... oh, Wilkes
ran the name. Still working that out." He looked curiously at
Garrick. "The train incident..."

Garrick nodded. "That was me."

"Of course it was." Another long pause settled as they
marshalled their thoughts. "So far nothing from their
mobiles either. I can see how some perv can take a pluck a
poor kid from a busy shopping centre, but two grown adults?
That's weird."

Garrick squinted as the ECG tone changed and he swore
there was a movement behind her closed eyelids. He took a
step closer. Lord hadn't noticed as he mused aloud.

"Chib called in a K9 unit to search the centre. We think
they're still there and it's a big old place." Garrick threw him a
look of intrigue, encouraging Lord to voice his thoughts. "A

fire evacuation, a bloody motorbike chase inside. It sounds like some elaborate distraction to take them. I mean, Fanta would have been an unexpected item in the bagging area, so to speak, but..."

As he trailed off, Garrick caught a definite flicker in Sonia's eyes. Her blood pressure rose a few points and a weak breath escaped her lips. Lord tensed.

"I'll get the nurse."

Garrick held up his hand to stop him. "Wait a sec." He leaned in close to Sonia's ear, which was wrapped in blood-stained bandages. "Sonia," he whispered.

Another faint gasp. On the ECG screen, her heart rate stepped up. Garrick gently held her hand.

"It's alright. We're all here. You can talk to us."

"Garrick..." there was a note of caution in Lord's voice.

Garrick threw him a sharp look, then turned back to Sonia.

"You're doing fine, sweetheart. Come and say hello. We all want to hear you." Interrogating a suspect who is half-unconscious violated protocol, but Garrick was grasping at straws and with the fate of Wendy and his unborn child at stake, he was willing to throw out the rule book.

Sonia's swollen eyelids opened a fraction. The whites of her eye were glossy, bloodshot, and unfocused. She tried to speak, her tongue brushing parched lips. Garrick quickly poured a cup of water from the plastic jug next to the bedside. He glanced at Lord who stood uneasily by the door, throwing occasional looks to the corridor. With care, Garrick tilted the cup, gently letting her sip the water.

"That's it. You'll be fine."

The water invigorated Sonia, and she attempted to move. Her pulse increased and her eyes lolled from side to side.

"Don't try to move. You've had an accident and you're pretty smashed up. Can you speak?"

Her lips parted with a gasp. "Where am I?" it was no more than a whisper, more akin to murmuring in her sleep.

"You're in hospital. Do you remember what happened?"

Her eyes rolled to the ceiling, but she didn't answer.

"Do you know who I am?"

When her gaze fell to him, he saw the colour had been washed away. It was as if he were gazing into the dead eyes of a shark. A cold, calculated killer. The hint of a smile tugged her cheeks.

"I know you..."

"Good. Where is Wendy?" The eyelids flickered in recognition. "Where is Fanta Liu?"

"You've been a bad lad, Davy..." she hissed with discernible contempt.

"Where are they?"

"A baby on the way too... she wanted to call her Clara..."

It felt as if an electric jolt sparked through Garrick. He and Wendy had discussed names, guessed on the sex, and even fantasised about their future career, but no names had been settled upon, and here was Sonia, stranger, a cuckoo who had jimmied her way into their lives and now was spouting privileged information. He felt murderous.

But what stuck the knife into Garrick was her use of the past tense.

It was a psychological battle to keep his voice level. "Where are they? This is not a game, Sonia."

Her pulse spiked, and she smiled. "But it is. And one you're losing," she croaked.

Garrick's mind accelerated in overtime. Sonia had deliberately inserted herself into their lives, whether Duncan

Cook had been part of it, or she had seduced and beguiled him into the cult's twisted cause was irrelevant. He had assumed the chase would end with her, the sole surviving deviant who had been extending John Howard's twisted game. But he was wrong.

He ran his fingers down the IV line that led to the dorsal arch veins on the back of her hand. Yanking it out would be painful... but she was so dosed up with morphine that she'd never feel the punishment. A pillow over her face would be too subtle a death.

Garrick moved his hand away from the plastic tube. As much as he wanted to, he couldn't allow himself to descend to their depths. They may have gnawed at his mental health, punished him psychically and emotionally, but he still had his morals. Even if that was the one last aspect of his former self that he could cling to. If they took that away, they would have won.

"Where are they?" he repeated, his voice lowering with threatened menace.

Sonia replied with a dismissive hiss. Garrick's fists balled as he controlled his rage. He inhaled a stuttering breath, only just managing to calm himself. *Fight fire with fire.* He leaned in close to Sonia's damaged ear and whispered.

"Duncan's dead." Sonia's sharp intake of breath was all he needed to confirm they were indeed connected. A dark sense of glee overtook him. "I killed him, Sonia. The cottage burned down, and he ran. Jumped on a train and," he drew his finger across his throat and make a swishing sound, "His head came clean off when I shoved him out of the window." The ECG spiked and Sonia's eyes squinted as thick tears formed. "All that blood. It ruined my jacket."

"Bastard..." she could barely get the words out.

"Well, it's only a game, after all. You'll be dead soon enough. And I will have won. Think about all your lot scattered in morgues around the world. An army of sick, incompetent *cults* who couldn't even stop me."

Her left hand clenched and unclenched repeatedly in the only sign of frustration her broken body could give. Garrick patted it.

"Relax. I don't need you. You're nothing. You never were."

He turned and slowly headed for the door. He was almost across the threshold and into the corridor when he heard Sonia's raspy wheeze.

"Wait..."

Garrick smirked to himself. Questioning Sonia would have merely allowed her to taunt him by withholding information. He knew she was desperate to be portrayed as superior. Allowing him to walk out of the room left her with nothing but time to die alone.

He stopped and glanced back.

"I won't see you again. Ever." He forced a smile. "Close your eyes, Sonia. It's time to die." He motioned to turn away.

"She took her!"

Garrick threw her a dubious look.

"What trash are you talking about now? We know exactly where she is."

To his surprise, Sonia chuckled. It was an irritating sound. He took several steps back towards her. The ECG was rising in pace with each passing moment.

"She was right about you. Arrogant. A know-it-all. You're a dirty person. People like you shouldn't be allowed to live. And she won't let you. She wants to be found. And I know where she is."

"It doesn't matter."

Sonia gave two grunts of frustration. Her words came with more effort than before. "Come closer and I'll tell you."

Garrick glanced at DC Lord who had been quietly observing from beyond the doorway. What could a half-dead woman do to him? He walked across.

"Closer," she whispered barely on the cusp of hearing. When Garrick didn't budge, she added, "I'll tell you where they are. Come closer."

Garrick leaned in so her ear was centimetres away from her mouth. This close he could see the shattered teeth, no more than jagged fangs, injuries sustained from the crash. Garrick resisted the urge to pull away. He reminded himself that Sonia was a broken woman, on the threshold of death and unable to move.

DC Harry Lord frowned as she whispered to Garrick. He took a step inside the room as Garrick sharply pulled his head away, his face drained of colour.

"You okay, Guv?" Harry said.

Garrick had trouble tearing his gaze away from Sonia, who now looked genuinely pleased with herself.

"Now you know."

"Where are they?" Lord asked, concerned with Garrick's sudden reaction. Sonia answered for him.

"He knows. He knows everything now. Don't you, Davy?"

A husky laugher rolled from the back of her phellem coated throat. It was a sound that seemed distant and alien to Garrick.

2 ^{5}

IMPULSE WAS the wrong instinct to follow if you wanted to stay alive.

Garrick knew this. It fuelled improvisation, which was the mother of accident. Now he found himself throwing caution to the wind as his focused narrowed to a single prime directive.

Save them.

With Sonia's grunting syphilitic laughter ringing in his ears, Garrick shouldered past Lord in his haste to leave.

"Guv?"

Garrick ignored him as he jogged towards the closing elevator door ahead. His legs felt like lead, and a sharp pain shot up his left-hand side with each jolting step.

"David!?" Lord yelled after him in desperation.

Garrick was through the closing doors, leaving him with the last glimpse of DC Harry Lord standing halfway down the corridor, throwing a confused look between his fleeing boss and the doorway to Sonia's ward, which he was supposed to guard.

Garrick slumped in the corner of the elevator, his hands trembling, and his eyes half hooded as he tried to work out a game plan. He saw a young nurse in blue scrubs glance at him with concern, but she kept silent and as far away from him as possible. He guessed he looked like some sort of derange patient making his escape. The elevator stopped at the next floor, where she made a hasty exit. Garrick's brooding presence ensured nobody else entered the car.

The clock was ticking, and he was in an impossible bind. He had to make a ninety-minute drive south as quickly as possible to the East Sussex coast. But he had no car, no phone and was, technically, still dead. He had to trust what Sonia had told him was the truth. The irony of trusting a collective of liars was palpable, but the sadistic intent was clear, so he had no reason to doubt her.

He reached for his phone. It wasn't in his pocket. He patted his jacket down and found his wallet, but no phone. Then he remembered Kane had taken it, explaining that the moment he switched it on, those lurking in the shadows would know he was alive. Garrick felt oddly naked without his phone. It was an oddly twenty-first century experience, or rather a modern-day handcuff. He'd left DC Lord without a word, fearing that the slightest whiff of official police involvement would make the precarious situation even worse. Sonia had made it clear that this was a personal matter.

The elevator doors closed, and he continued his descent.

He tried to put the jigsaw together. How his relationship with John Howard had turned into a deadly game. There was no doubt in his mind that Howard had intentionally befriended him. The serial killer had already started his cult-like Murder Club since his days as a soldier in the Falklands Conflict. The passing years saw him increase his network of like-minded sociopaths who emerged from their sordid pits across every level of society, bound by the same fascination for death and pain.

As far as he could tell, Garrick had been chosen as an experiment to subvert an honest cop. Testing how far he could be pushed both morally and mentally. An experiment that had started with the calculated murder of his sister, Emilie. He could never tell how much their previous victims had been tormented, but Garrick had reached breaking point several times. Even after John Howard's death, the plot unwound towards this very moment. He was about to face his final adversary, and the lives of those he held dearest were at stake. He'd been a bachelor for so long during his career that he never thought he'd really fall in love, never mind start a family. Then Wendy had entered his life and his world had changed...

Coincidence...

Garrick never believed in coincidences. During any investigation, they were a warning sign that something was wrong. Premeditated. Yet, it appeared that coincidences believed in *him* as they kept cropping up. John Howard... Sergeant Howard. What were the odds? That point had been compounded with the murder of David Garrick in Illinois. It was difficult to conceive that all these coincidences had really been engineered to mess with his mind, yet that's where the evidence pointed.

As the elevator car jogged to a stop on the ground floor, Garrick was consumed by doubt and anxiety. Who could he really trust? Could he even trust himself now that he was flying solo into the very meat grinder John Howard had started so long ago?

The doors opened, and he stepped out, almost shouldering aside an orderly who was some magnitude bigger than him. He muttered an apology and looked around to get his bearings and find the exit.

DC Harry Lord blocked his path, doubled over with his hands on his knees as he gasped for breath.

"You made me..." he sucked in a deep breath, "run down those bloody stairs..." he patted his leg. "This is a lame bastard." He now sported a permanent leg injury, sustained in the line of duty with Garrick when he'd been run over by a fleeing suspect. He straightened up, sucking in a great lungful of air. "So, where are we going?"

Garrick held up both hands. "Harry, mate, please. This is my mess. I've gotta do this alone." He tried to step aside, but Harry blocked him.

"How long have we known each other?"

Harry was one of Garrick's oldest friends, in a world where he had few people that he could claim he was close to. They'd been regular constables on the street before Garrick had become a detective and, later, Harry had chosen that career path too.

Garrick expelled an exasperated sigh. "That's not the point, Harry. This has got very dirty. Officially, I'm not here. This'll ruin your career. Mine's already in tatters." He cocked his head to the side in a bullish manner. The bones cricked alarmingly. "You're not standing in my way."

DC Harry Lord pulled a face. "That's what you think of me? Really?" He pulled out his police warrant card and held it up for Garrick to see. Then he theatrically tossed it into a nearby rubbish bin. It bounced off the side and slid under a blue plastic bucket seat. Unperturbed, he continued. "I'm not a cop today." Then he fished his car keys from his pants' pocket. "And you're going to need this."

Despite the tension searing through his shoulder muscles, Garrick managed a smile.

"You're gonna get fired for this."

Harry gave a dismissive snort. "After all, we've done for King and country. Let them try." He nodded his head towards the exit. "Let's go."

Garrick patted him on the shoulder, and they walked towards the sliding entrance door. Harry suddenly stopped and backtracked. He crouched and retrieved his warrant card from under the chair. Embarrassed, he waggled it at Garrick before slipping it into his pocket.

"I shouldn't really leave this lying around. That's unprofessional."

ONCE GARRICK HAD GIVEN him the destination, Harry Lord drove in companionable silence. Garrick toyed with his phone. It was still switched off. It took a leap of faith to believe they were heading in the right direction. It could be a wild goose chase designed to part him and Wendy further, but he doubted it. All he had to do was turn his phone on and call her to check. But *if* the Murder Club still thought he was dead, turning on his phone may warn them he was on his way. He was in a bind that ultimately hinged on how much he trusted a pathological killer who had threaded her way into his life. He hadn't given many details to Harry, other than their final destination, and Harry was wise enough not to ask. Garrick had eked out a promise that Harry could stay in the car no matter what.

They had turned off the M25 and onto the slower A21 towards Eastbourne in East Sussex. Harry drove like a demon, but there was a limit to how far he could bully his way through the traffic without risking injuring somebody. Garrick impatiently tapped the dashboard as they passed through Tunbridge Wells and he fixated on the office of his private physician, Doctor Rajasekar, who had saved his life by diagnosing his tumour and arranging the fast-track surgery. Fat raindrops suddenly obscured the window, and the squeak of broken window wipers jolted him to the road ahead. A deluge was suddenly upon them. Harry waited until they'd navigated out of the town and onto the steep A26 before he spoke again.

"Maybe we should call Chib–"

"No!" Garrick snapped louder than he'd meant to. Harry got the point, but pressed on.

"Or Wilkes. If Fanta is involved in this–"

"Harry. No. Sonia said blood would be shed the moment I alerted anybody to what was going on. Even you coming with me is a risk."

"But Fanta–"

Despite their constant bickering, Harry was fond of the young DC and was always monitoring her. They'd nearly lost her once, and he knew that pain had affected the team hard, particularly DC Sean Wilkes. The two of them were dating. Possibly even living together.

But now the table had dramatically changed, and Garrick didn't want to think about anything other than Wendy's safety. He'd ran through many scenarios in his head, and in each one he was confident that he could kill to protect her. Perhaps that's what John Howard had intended all along; to turn him into a killer. In that case, Garrick was happy to lose if it brought an end to his torment.

Harry gave a sharp sigh, and his fingers clenched the steering wheel a little tighter.

"Chib will go nuclear if you go behind her back."

Detective Sergeant Chibarameze Okon had been assigned to his team undercover, at the behest of DCI Kane. At the time, it had been a traumatic revelation and one that had seriously damaged the team's trust in her. When she had the opportunity to return to the MET, she declined and had asked Garrick if she could stay with him. It was a testament to her bloody-mined determination that she done so and earned the respect of her colleagues. However, that didn't mean she would play along with a round of severe rule-breaking. Chib was somebody who played by the book, even under extreme circumstances. Letting her know what was happening would trigger a disaster.

"Harry, let it go. She would deal with this by the playbook. And that's going to get Wendy killed."

Harry threw him a concerned look, but lapsed into silence. He might not approve, but he was a man of his word and he'd stick by Garrick no matter what. The rain continued blurring the windscreen as they took the dark country roads. Garrick glanced at the clock and felt a sudden wave of fatigue as he registered that it was approaching six in the morning. He'd been awake all night in the hospital and now that he needed to stay sharp, he was overwhelmed by sleep. He couldn't resist closing his eyes. His head gently lolled against the passenger window as the combination of creaking window wipers and the car engine sang a soporific song.

Their destination loomed in his mind. Beachy Head.

The country's capital for suicides as people threw themselves off the White Cliffs of Dover. And now it was his last stand.

26

2 ⁶

DAVID GARRICK OPENED HIS EYES. It was the gentle rocking from the car as Lord pulled into the West Car Park. He blinked and rubbed his eyes. It was still raining heavily as the wind blew in from the English Channel. It brought with it a cloak of mist that choked the dawn, instead casting everything in a monochromatic shroud.

"I had to break the gate open," Harry explained. "I don't think there's anybody here." He cut the engine, and they listened to the tattoo of rain. The cliff offered few places to hide. From the car park, the hill gently rolled upwards, offering a deceptive sense of safety before the cliffs and the one-hundred-sixty-two metre drop to the rocky shoreline below.

Garrick put his hand on the door latch. "Well, I suppose

we'll find out. Stay here. No matter what. If Wendy turns up. Go. Don't wait for me."

Harry gave a single solemn nod. Garrick opened the door and clambered out. The sleep had done wonders to clear his head, and the sting of the rain was an invigorating slap across the face. He hunched forward to counter the constant breeze and walked towards the cliff edge as he'd been instructed.

The location was synonymous with death, and Garrick knew the end plan was that nobody would be walking away alive. He knew that was never the intention. The Murder Club cult didn't consist of nihilists. They had every intention of living to a ripe old age, but Garrick took some satisfaction that he had whittled their numbers down to one. The sole survivor of John Howard's legacy. Sonia hadn't revealed the name, but Garrick had patched the pieces together since he'd arrived in Flora. All along he had been thinking far too small, probing each individual element, and stress-testing his theories as he would in any other investigation. Which is exactly how his opponents assumed he worked. For a few years, John Howard had a chance to talk to Garrick. Lull him into a false sense of friendship. They even discussed cases, and Howard had been particularly useful in solving several of them. Only in retrospect did Garrick wonder if John Howard hadn't simply set-up or betrayed members of his own cult to see how a seasoned detective would take the bait. And he had taken then bait, over-and-over.

It was only when he took a step back. No longer taking in every strand of evidence the Club had laid because they were designed to be seen that way. That was the revelation Garrick had experienced in the States. He was playing by their rules. Examining a picture they had crafted and therefore, he was following clues they had planted. It was like a four-dimensional chess game, with evidence and suggestions pointing in various directions to add an element of randomness. Only with retrospect and scrutiny did Garrick see that it was such an element of randomness that had derailed their plans and led to John Howard being exposed along with the other members of the collective.

Despite this, he had followed the clues to this very point. Exactly as they had designed. He felt a flush of envy that Agent Rivera could pack a sidearm. He wouldn't hesitate to blow his assailant away at the very first sight. But at least he was armed with something just as useful. Knowledge of the way they think.

He had been looking at the threads and clues. The moment he stopped to think about what *wasn't there*, a different picture emerged. Looking into the negative space, into the void where existing clues curled around facts or diverted attention to the shiny thing. John Howard's plan had been a masterclass in illusions. Only allowing Garrick to see what he wanted to see. Like an optical illusion where he had thought he'd been looking at a flower vase, only to realise it was a pair of faces looking at one another.

The last surviving member of the cult had been in front of him all along. Watching him. Learning from him. Knowing just how he ticked. The culprit had been part of the illusion.

The damp grass was seeping into his cheap trainers, and his socks were already sodden. He slipped on a muddy patch and his heart leapt into his mouth at the thought of blindly stumbling over the edge to his doom before he could rescue Wendy.

Ahead, a dark shadow appeared in the mist. It had a hunched-like quality and staggered, making him alert to the proximity of the cliff edge. This was the worst weather and worst time of day to be here. It was as if it was all by design.

"Stop there!" he called out, his voice taken by the wind.

The figure ignored him and continued forward. Garrick tensed and glanced around. This was a rendezvous by design. There was no way they could have seen him coming in the mist, which meant he had been watched from afar, but how in such atrocious weather? He stopped and waited for the figure to approach. He'd deliberately come unarmed. The rules of such engagements were well established, so raising his arms and emptying his pockets of hidden weaponry was an act of theatre he had no time for.

On the very edge of perception, the mist gave way just enough so he could see who it was.

"Wendy!" her name was almost choked by the tears welling within him.

She stopped. He could see her eyes were wide with fear and a black leather strap gagged her. Both arms were held behind her back and Garrick noticed a handcuff around her ankle was linked to somebody behind her.

He addressed his hidden antagonist with more confidence than he felt. "This is it. This is what you wanted. But it will not end the way you want it to. You're in the same boat as me. You have nowhere to go. Nowhere to hide." He pointed at Wendy. "She's coming with me, and there's nothing you can do to stop me."

He took a step – but Wendy's head snapped back, and she gave a frightened squeal. Garrick stopped, his bravado flushing away.

"It's going to be okay. I've got this covered." He wasn't trying to assure Wendy, he was trying to psyche-out his opponent.

Behind Wendy, somebody moved. It was an awkward movement because their ankles were cuffed together. Garrick squinted. His heart racing as the familiar face came into view. It wasn't what he was expecting. He'd long danced around the notion that John Howard had faked his own death and planted a corpse at his burning house for just such an inevitability, but there had been no solid evidence. Just speculation. He had been a phantom... but more than that, the thought of him being alive had been the distraction.

Garrick's mouth went dry, and he couldn't find his voice. He croaked the words.

"Fanta...?"

DC Fanta Liu looked at Garrick with tears in her eyes.

27

2⁷

A FURIOUS WIND suddenly drove the tempest harder as the three figures gathered. Garrick's eyes were fixed on Fanta and Wendy. The fog next to them churned, hinting at the edge of the cliff mere steps away.

"What are you doing, Fanta?"

She shook her head, tears in her eyes. It was then Garrick switched to logical mode. Fanta was shackled to Wendy by their right ankles to prevent them running. Even if they tried, they'd only manage a shuffle, which explained Wendy's awkward gait. Wendy's hands remained behind her back, and only when Fanta took another step could he see they were bound by the wrists, too. Gagged, they could give no warning or explanation. But as Fanta took another step aside from Wendy, Garrick saw something truly horrific. She wore a khaki sleeveless military vest that had seen better days. The fabric was dirty and torn to accommodate wires that had been threaded around the straps, affixed to a series of tubes. It looked like a hastily constructed suicide vest.

"Is that a bomb?" he asked, licking his suddenly dry lips. Fanta nodded. "I'll get it off."

He took a step forward – prompting both women to howl a muffled, yet obvious, "NO!" Fanta stepped back, almost bringing Wendy down on top of her.

Garrick's mind was racing. They couldn't move, and he was certain if he did something awful would happen. Yet he refused to stand idle and play along. He slowly circled them, moving away from the edge of the cliff. He lowered his voice.

"Do nothing. I'm going to get you out of this."

"And how are you going to do that?" came a woman's voice from the air. It took Garrick several seconds to realise there was a phone strapped to Fanta's vest. The screen was dimmed, but the line active.

"I see you're playing a coward's game. At least John Howard had the guts to reveal himself."

A mocking snigger came from the phone. "John was a genius, but overly sentimental. I miss him. We all do. He was a generous man."

Garrick could hardly reconcile the crazy woman's description with the serial killer. Her flippancy angered him.

"He was a dickhead who deserved to die. And he did. Like all the others. You think you're so smart? Hiding in the shadows? Ha, anybody can do that."

He took a step closer but stopped when the woman gave a sharp, "No! No closer or the three of you explode in a beautiful suicide pact."

Fanta and Wendy's agitation increased. Garrick glanced

around. So their tormentor could see them. Perhaps through the phone on the camera, but he wasn't convinced. Raindrops had splattered across the entire surface, so the lens would be blurred.

"I don't believe you'd go to all this effort and do that. I don't even believe that it's a real explosive." He took another step closer. Wendy and Fanta shuffled backwards – towards the edge of the cliff. Garrick stopped.

"You'd be willing to take that chance? Fascinating."

Garrick held out his hand towards the women. "Stop moving. You're near the edge. She won't do anything."

He met their gaze as best as he could in the grey light. They were frightened and desperate to trust him. That was painful to Garrick. How could they trust him when he didn't trust himself? He was eying the phone. That was probably the remote detonator. If he could remove it, then perhaps he could disable the bomb. But he was no explosives expert. By removing the phone, he had just as much chance as triggering it.

The odds were fifty-fifty. But what were the odds playing this insane woman's game? He was sure they were stacked in her favour. Which made fifty-fifty the most favourable odds. Wendy was holding together well, but he doubted she was so calm and collected underneath. Fanta was used to high-pressure situations, and he hoped this one hadn't broken her. He held Fanta's gaze.

"Where is she?"

"You're wasting your time," came the voice as Fanta steadily looked towards the second parking area.

"Is she still there?"

Fanta gave the slightest nod.

"Stop talking to them," the woman barked.

Garrick considered his next steps. He could charge forward and removed the phone, hoping it wouldn't trigger a detonation – if indeed the explosives were real. Or he could run through the fog, and hopefully out of sight, towards the car park, hoping to reach the woman. If he did that, he suspected his tormentor would detonate the explosives out of malice.

"Why are you doing this?" Garrick asked as he stalled for time, hoping a plan would form. He now regretted telling Harry Lord to stay behind.

"Simple. I hate you."

If she was in the other car park, then surely she would know Lord was here too. It was a difficult task to hide the only car on the single road stretching the length of the cliffs.

"You don't know me," he replied on autopilot. His attention was firmly on the immediate dilemma. The women were chained together. There would be no quick and easy slash of a rope.

"I know you better than you know yourself."

"Sure..." he said dismissively as he slowly paced back around Wendy and Fanta, holding up his hand to indicate they shouldn't move. The wires on the vest led to a small black oblong that looked like a portable phone battery. If he removed the power, then the bomb couldn't detonate... could it?

The woman's taunts continued as he tried to work out what to do. "You're thinking why did you tell Harry to stay in the car? Why isn't he coming to your aid? I mean, when did he ever follow the rules?"

Although he wasn't paying attention, the words suddenly struck like a dagger in his brain. How did she know? That conversation happened in the car. Unless she had already planted a bug, or–

A terrific explosion suddenly lit up the car park as Harry Lord's car exploded with such fury that it lifted off the ground, the centre of the chassis buckling into a V-shape as it crashed back down. The shockwave from the explosion rippled towards them, visible as it distorted the layers of mist. Garrick felt the deep bass blast shake his chest.

Garrick was stunned. She had killed his friend. He was about to unleash a torrent of abuse at the killer, when a dazzling full beam headlight suddenly pierced the gloom, almost blinding him. He squinted, using his fingers as a shade so he could get a better look. It was a white Jeep. The lack of engine noise meant it was electric and had stealthily made its way parallel to the cliff edge to reach them. If it sped up in a straight line, it would run Fanta and Wendy over.

His options had dwindled almost to zero. Once again, he was caught in her game. Her rules. Which meant her outcome was even more likely. With a soft click, the driver's door opened, and a woman stepped out.

"It was all my idea really," she said, this time shouting over the wind and rain. "John was amazing. When I met him, it was like meeting Charles Manson for the first time. I was such a fan girl."

He could see she was short. Five-six, perhaps. Physically, she was no match against him. That meant she was confident she held the power over Wendy and Fanta. She held a mobile phone in her right hand. The screen was illuminated. Garrick tried to process the accent. It was familiar; he was sure there was some Liverpool scouse in there somewhere.

She continued. "So when I talked to him about you, he was fascinated. He saw you for what you are. A dirty, nasty cockroach I wanted to stamp for so long. But he came up with the plan on how to test you. A series of measures designed to break the most hardened son-of-a bitch. Because that's what you are."

Impatiently, Garrick took a step towards her. She raised the phone in one hand and wagged a finger. "Ah, ah. No, you don't or you'll be seeing your baby's guts all over the White Cliffs."

Bile and hatred swelled in Garrick's stomach, but he held his ground.

"And so it began. The grand project designed to crack you and wear you down one piece at a time."

"Who are you?"

"You really are a terrible detective, Detective Garrick. I'm the one who has hated you my whole life. As a child, I dreamed of killing you, and now this is a testament that dreams really can come true if you believe hard enough."

"Just release them and I can get you psychological help. All the help you need. And this," he indicated Wendy, "We can forget all about it. In the grand scheme of things, it's not important."

The woman laughed. "There you go. That's what I remember. The arrogance. The incessant lies. The reason you don't know who I am is because you've *never* paid attention to me. All this time I was nothing to you. I knew John's ideas on how to strip away your sins, your misguided virtue, or stubbornness. Then I'd have to make a grand statement to get your attention. The question is, do I still have your attention?"

She stepped out from behind the car door and was illuminated by the Jeep's full beams. Garrick gasped and dropped to his knees. That amused the woman.

"I suppose I do, Davy." She extended her arms like a showman. "Here I am. Breathe it in."

Garrick now knew why the accent was so familiar. He felt paralysed as the entire world around him slotted into place. But he wasn't looking at the picture, he was gazing into the negative space. And the woman in front of him was a very familiar face who had stepped from the voids of negative space and presented herself to him.

The craziness had come full circle.

She winked at Garrick. "Hi *Davy*. Miss me?"

2 [8]

"WHAT WAS THAT QUOTE? Reports of my death were... yadda, yadda, yadda," said Emilie Garrick.

"Em?" He dropped to his knees in exhaustion. "How...?" His voice was barely audible over the rain.

Emilie regarded her older brother with scorn. She stepped around the car, ensuring he didn't miss a single syllable of her victory speech.

"We were always opposites, Davy. You remember that? You were the apple of our parents' eye. And me... the disappointment."

Garrick shook his head, tears rolling down his cheeks. "That's not true. I was the one who left home. I never got on with dad."

"Neither did I! You left me there when you were supposed

to protect me."

Images of their childhood flashed through his mind. Emilie was the unsmiling child, filled with teen angst. She had even poisoned his beloved aquarium out of spite, killing every colourful tropical fish. He couldn't recall a single moment of light and joy, just conflict and arguments.

Emilie moved closer, peering down at her brother with unbridled scorn. Every day I got to watch the contempt in your eyes.

Garrick shook his head. "That's not true…"

Emilie dismissively waved the hand holding her phone. "Don't worry. I don't need sympathy. I can look after myself. I did. Thank God for the Dark Web. I found John's website selling all sorts of freaky things. Books bound in human flesh. How sick is that?" She giggled. "And I mean *sick,* meaning *good.* So I reached out to him to see if I could help." She nodded, smiling at the memory. "Now there was a father figure I needed. Somebody to look up to. Somebody who saw me as a person to love. And there were others. An entire society of people around the world who needed an outlet for their feelings. Who all needed one another."

"Don't you see this is all wrong? Civilisations can't function like that. You're sick Emilie."

Her smile vanished. She stood up and paced to the side, positioning Garrick between her and the cliff edge. "I don't think you mean *sick* in the nice way. Typical you. John was fascinated by human behaviour. Only by dismantling a thing can you learn how it works. That includes people. He believed by understanding how to break people, we could improve society." Her voice lowered and was almost lost in the wind. "He was a visionary."

"He was a psychopath," Garrick snapped back.

Emilie's expression darkened. "That's what people like you don't understand. He did. When I told him about you, he saw that I'd given him a great challenge. A person who thinks he's so superior and incorruptible, who's really a man we know is a complete uncaring bastard." She pointed. "That's you. Brought down to a base level. Tested and tease and eventually stripped down to this: a pathetic man grovelling on his knees."

Garrick shook his head and indicated Wendy and Fanta. "They're not part of this. Let them go."

"Of course they're part of it, you moron! Haven't you seen Pinocchio?"

Garrick looked up at her. Rain stung his eyes as it dripped off his brow. He blinked the drops away. Emilie was really enjoying herself, behaving as if she was delivering a performance to a bunch of school kids. "Jiminy Cricket was the grasshopper. Pinocchio's conscience. That's what they are. And like him, a conscience is a bug to crush. That is the psychological anchor that holds us all back. We don't need something in here," she tapped her head, "to make us feel bad. What function is served by dwelling on past decisions? None."

Not empathy. No desire to learn from mistakes. Emilie was a textbook psychopath, already several rungs up from a sociopath. She smiled and extended her arms to the sky, enjoying the rain seeping through her blue plastic raincoat and jeans. Then she turned her gaze onto Garrick and smiled pleasantly.

"I wouldn't waste your breath trying to convince me to let them go. That would be stupid. They're going to die. Along with my little niece." She winked at Wendy. "Who wants that family line to carry on? No. The question is all about timing. The anticipation of it all."

"Em, whatever John Howard told you, he lied. He has been manipulating you from the very beginning. All this hatred you're feeling isn't because of me. It's because of *him*. He's used you to become the very thing you claim to hate."

"Now that is armchair psychology, Davy. I know what I like. I enjoy toying with you. Getting in your head and tinkering around. I enjoy bringing you down one emotional beat at a time. I like to see how people react to pain. It's fascinating."

"What happened to you at the ranch? What did they do to break you?"

Emilie's eye widened. "In the States? No, you've got your timeline mixed up. The ranch was supposed to be the launch pad to go after you. Our special project. We were all there." Her voice was filled with childlike wonder. "It was like a secret society, but better. Something we could really belong to. I was trying to work out a way to bring Sam in. He was a nice bloke. Hell, we were getting married. But you don't want to marry the wrong person. You need somebody with things you have in common. You've met Maureen back in Flora. Happily married, but always regretted having to keep a secret from her hubby. I didn't want that. I wanted Sam on the inside."

"Like your little power couple, Sonia and Duncan?" That struck a nerve. Emilie snarled.

"That bastard was a loose end. He'd fallen for Sonia in a big way. Would do anything for her, the little freak. Sonia is *mine*."

Garrick knew proving his sister was the wrong thing to do, but the older brother instinct overrode common sense.

"*Was*. She'll be dead by now."

Emilie lapsed into silence for a movement. Her fists clenched as she looked around, running the frigid rainwater across his face. Garrick glanced at Wendy and Fanta. They hadn't moved. Rooted to the spot, they stared at Emilie – the star freak in the freak show.

"Dear Sam was a loose end," she eventually said. "When he found out he turned on us. Boy, he had a temper." She shook her head. "Who wants to be in a relationship with an abusive husband? Not me. He tried to free the others we'd rounded up." Garrick frowned as her face flickered. Was it a hint of buried emotion? "Between you and me, I think he had the hots for that Korean medical student. They turned on us. Almost killed poor old John. And me? Jeez. I had to run for my life. That was scary." She held up her hand and Garrick noticed the missing fingers. "That's when I lost these in the line of duty. Stuck in a door! I had to hack them off or..." she shook her head. "Well. They were a lynch mob. I should've known. On the way there, we almost ran over a guy who had escaped. Luckily, I was able to take him back. That was Grant's fault. He messed up security in a big way." She shrugged. "Anyway, all good things, right? We realised that having me dead was the ideal place to be if I wanted to wear you down. It wasn't a plan. It was an opportunity that I think worked out rather well."

"Rather well? It got John Howard killed."

Emilie shrugged. "And I miss him. But the one thing John taught me was happiness lies within the self." She placed a palm against her chest. "This is what counts. The rest of the world is just accessories."

Garrick blinked against the full-beam headlights of the car. Emilie had left them switched on to illuminate her stage.

They were dazzling, but Garrick swore he caught movement behind them.

Emilie didn't see him as a threat. All she saw was a broken man she was bursting to lecture. For all her talk of breaking people down to see what makes them tick, she had fallen for her own trap. Arrogance and pride had been the lures that lowered her guard and fuelled her desire to monologue her perceived genius. After all, why go through such an elaborate act of revenge if the target is unaware of the care and attention crafted in such a plot.

That she was alive was no serious surprise. He had suspected that from the first day in Flora. Admittedly, the hatred and mechanics behind it were pure guess work, but from the trail of DNA clues – found on the empty envelope sent to him, the specks of blood found in the car in New York, which he now realised was because *she* was fleeing for her life from the very people they'd gathered to butcher – it all pointed at the fact. He even saw her disguised as a nurse when he went in for surgery. Was she that brazen, or had he been a victim of hallucination, as he'd thought?

Either way, it was irrelevant. Now was not the time to deconstruct timelines or confirm evidence or motives. The only thing that was important was the lives of Wendy, Fanta, and his unborn daughter. Killing Harry Lord indicated the suicide vest around Fanta was deadly, but he doubted Emilie would detonate it while she was in close proximity. That gave him a microscopic edge to wrest it from her control while they were all still together. The moment they were separated by any distance... the explosives could detonate and kill them all.

The odds were stacked in Emilie's favour.

He had to act now.

Emilie was mustering her thoughts for another delivery of superiority. Garrick coiled like a spring – then he bolted forwards. He crossed the space between them in seconds, wrapping one hand around her waist – the other groping for the phone, which he assumed was the detonator. He poured in every ounce of strength to crush her. She screeched as her fingers pressed hard against the phone's unyielding metal case and he angled her to take his full weight as they crashed to the ground. Even over the noise of the storm he heard her ribs crack. She tried to speak, but the breath was expelled from of her lungs.

He attempted to free his right arm to snatch the phone from her grip without shifting his weight; that would allow her to wriggle free. He tried to butt her in the face, but he was too awkwardly positioned.

Emilie squirmed, then planted a knee firmly in his groin. Garrick was already in a world of pain, but it still made him slump enough for her to slide on the wet grass and slip from under his crushing weight.

Their movements had drawn them to the very edge of the cliff and Garrick was suddenly looking straight down into a sea of grey. There was no sense of depth, and in the early, misty light the danger didn't feel real.

Emilie scrambled to her knees. Her face twisted in anger. Garrick rolled to his feet – and then knew the light was shifting around them. In his dazed state, he wasn't immediately certain what was happening. Then he understood. The Jeep was moving. The electric motor was imperceptible – but it was moving with some speed straight at them. It struck Emilie first, and she rolled onto the bonnet and thumped into the windscreen. Garrick tried to scramble aside, but he wasn't quick enough. The metal fender cracked into his hip with a searing pain – then he was thrown into the air and across the bonnet. Momentum caused him to roll straight into Emilie like a bizarre game of ten-pin bowling. Their combined weight shattered the windscreen – just as the Jeep went over the edge of Beachy Head cliff.

29

2⁹

ILLUSION AND MISDIRECTION had choked Garrick's world for far too long. It should have been no surprise to him that plummeting to his death would follow the same track.

In some places, the famous chalk cliffs had crumbled in huge vertical slabs, producing sheer drops. In other places, weather erosion was slowing wearing the surface away, creating steep plateaus. The electric jeep tipped over the edge of a sharp sixty-degree incline. Harry Lord was at the wheel, and his thoughts were far from suicidal. He had hoped to run Emilie over and come to a heroic stop. The wet, muddy grass and underlying chalk caused the vehicle to skid the moment the brakes locked.

Then it struck a boulder poised at the edge and came to a bone-jarring halt. Inside, Harry Lord struck the steering wheel. He was lucky that it prevented him from pitching headfirst through the broken windshield.

Garrick and Emilie were not so lucky.

As the car struck them, they were both hurled onto the bonnet and through the window. Glass shattered and they would have continued rolling into the Jeep's cabin – but the sudden change in incline forced them to roll back out of the vehicle and across the bonnet. The wet, slippery bonnet.

Garrick was in a world of pain, but his survival instincts were more alive than ever. He splayed his palms across the metal in a desperate attempt to stop his fall, but the incline was too steep, and the abrupt impact accelerated them. He was now twisting headfirst to be catapulted over the edge. He reached over the edge of the bonnet. His fingers found the crumpled metal of the bumper and tucked inside the buckled cracks. He tensed his arm and remarkably it slowed him to almost a complete stop before he tipped over the edge.

This happened within seconds. Emilie cannoned into him from behind and they both dropped off the edge of the bonnet with unified screams. With a crack, Garrick's fingers twisted and jammed in the narrow gap. Fortunately, it was a reenforced plastic bumper – a metal one would have severed his fingers. His body flipped over the edge so that he was facing out into a sea of mist. Pain surged through his arm, but that was nothing compared to the agony of his back as it smashed across the boulder which was anchoring the Jeep in place.

With a scream, Emilie shot overhead, her legs kicking and her hands gouging towards Garrick. One hand snagged his belt, the other his ankle – yanking her to a sudden stop and dislocating Garrick's arm in the process.

Garrick was arched around the boulder like a sacrificial

victim, his legs dangling over the edge and his sister clinging onto him for life. With all the weight suspended on one arm, Garrick felt the stitches from his recent stab wound pop as the wound tore open again. The mist chose that moment to part – revealing the sheer drop and the rocks below, which were being relentlessly beaten by the surging waves.

It also brought Emilie's face to sharp relief. Her eyes were alert and focused on him. For a moment, her emerald-green eyes reminded him of his little sister, the one before she became a truculent, troubled child. She regarded him with detachment. He couldn't discern an ounce of regret or hope. Just blank emotion.

This wasn't his sister. In his heart, she had died long ago. He had been grieving for somebody who didn't exist. A figment of hope, of what might have been. This woman was a fraud, a changeling brought into his life to ruin it. Even facing death, she barely reacted at a human level. Instead, she brought the phone up towards her face. She was so desperate to complete her evil path that she'd chosen to cling on to it rather than let it fall.

The car suddenly rocked as loose debris around its base crumbled under the weight. He heard Harry swear and move around in the vehicle. The rock would not support the car for much longer.

And at that point the decision was made in Garrick's mind. He had feared that the phone was some sort of dead man's switch which would detonate the suicide vest on Fanta the moment she let go. But her desire to cling on to it indicated she had to manually push a button. That one simple act would kill Wendy, the baby, and Fanta.

All he had to do was let go and they would both plunge to their death, saving the others. He had no choice.

DCI David Garrick relinquished his grip on the bumper.

But he didn't fall. Instead, a searing pain shot through the broken fingers wedged in the bumper's crack as they held their combined weight. He roared in agony. Emilie ignored his pain. It felt as if she was moving in slow motion as she angled the phone to her face so that facial recognition could unlock it.

"You win," Garrick snarled. She hesitated and looked at him with curiosity. "You've turned me into a killer."

With that, he slammed a boot into her face as hard as he could. He didn't stop pounding again and again, the cartilage in her nose breaking. With his other foot, he kicked the phone from her hand. He heard the shriek of frustration as it spiralled to the rocks below. Then her grip slipped, and she plummeted.

Garrick couldn't tear his eyes away as she silently fell. Her gaze never wavered from his until, mercifully, the mist rolled back in, swallowing her before she burst on the virgin white rocks below.

Garrick tensed, waiting for any sound from the cliff top above...

There was nothing but the blustering wind and the rain pinging from the car – which shook again. Garrick was numb, so he was hanging like a dummy, with no strength to pull himself up, and unable to slip to his death.

"David! Grab a hold!"

Garrick looked up. Harry had climbed out of the driver's side window and perched on the door sill. With one hand, he held onto to the door's pillion post as he stretched down with the other.

Garrick had been thinking about a quick death, but the thought of Wendy grieving and his daughter growing up without a father suddenly spurred him on. With an unplumbed surge of power, Garrick swung his free arm up – and Harry gripped it like a vice. Garrick could now flip himself around, so that he was no longer stretched across the rock.

"I got you! You're going to have to climb up."

Garrick didn't think he could, but his scrambling feet found purchase on the boulder. With an assist from Harry, he was able to clamber up onto the Jeep's bonnet. Now he had repositioned himself, his fingers easily slipped out of the hole in the bumper. He glanced at his bloodied and twisted hand.

The car suddenly shook.

"GO! GO!" Harry yelled, heaving Garrick upward so that he could find purchase on the Jeep's roof. No longer supporting his boss, Harry pulled himself free of the window, his shoes resting on the sill as the Jeep made a single violent lurch. They could hear rocks beginning to cascade from the boulder's base.

Then the anchoring rock rolled forward – pushed by the heavy vehicle. Harry leapt to the side, landing on the steep slope. He fell as flat as possible, grasping rocks and grass to prevent him from sliding after the car.

The car rolled from under Garrick. He ran several steps as the Jeep moved under him – then he was leaping for the incline as the Jeep rolled off the edge and became a violent tombstone for Emilie Garrick.

Garrick's limbs trembled as he held on to the side of the slope. The physical and emotional punishment had taken its toll. He had been forced to kill his sister. He would never know if this was ultimately John Howard's desire... but it didn't matter.

He was alive. Harry was alive, and on the cliff top above,

Fanta, Wendy and Clara had survived the ordeal, and that was all that counted. Life would return to some form of normality as it always did. His broken body would heal. Questions would be raised, but he was sure not too many would be answered.

He forced himself up the wet slope, his trainers slipping on the grass and mud, threatening to pull him back down, but he made it with relentless determination. Rolling onto the flat cliff, he finally took in a deep breath and cried as every form of emotion coursed through his system. When Harry made his way up, Garrick rolled on his side and offered a helping hand for the final ascent.

"My driving hasn't improved," Harry muttered. He wasn't expecting Garrick to appreciate the quip, but gallows humour was a long-standing tool in the copper's handbook to keep them sane.

With a grunt of effort, Garrick got to his feet. There was enough dawn light now to see Fanta and Wendy metres away. They both sobbed with delight to see him alive. Garrick limped forward and gave Wendy the tightest embrace he could remember.

"I love you..." he said through halting breaths. Because of being chained together, Fanta Liu had been pulled into the hug, too. He was fine with that... but less so the suicide belt she still wore.

There would be an enquiry. No doubt Molly Meyers would already be on a flight back to the UK to cover the extraordinary ending of her documentary. Garrick promised himself he'd have no part in it. DCI Kane was welcome to handle that. There would be countless unanswered questions. From how Emilie had travelled back to the UK. Her relationship with Sonia and her position in the Murder Club.

Garrick decided that he was happy to leave those answers hanging. He no longer cared. All he wanted to do was return to a normal life, although he knew the image of him forcing his sister to plunge to her death would live with him forever.

He'd just have to accept it. Just like he'd have to accept other things – that life was worth living. He kissed Wendy on the forehead and held her tight, taking in her warm, comforting scent. He reversed his earlier decision. Emilie hadn't won. He had.

And he would soon have a daughter to prove that life is worth living.

And DCI David Garrick, for one, would live his life to the full...

ALSO BY M.G. COLE

info@mgcole.com

or say hello on Twitter: @mgcolebooks

SIREN'S CALL

DCI Garrick 8- COMING SOON!

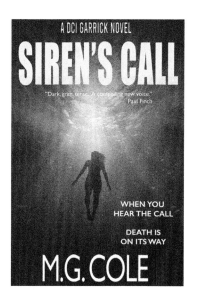

SLAUGHTER OF INNOCENTS

DCI Garrick 1

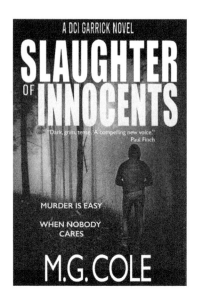

MURDER IS SKIN DEEP

DCI Garrick 2

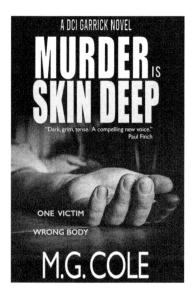

THE DEAD WILL TALK

DCI Garrick 3

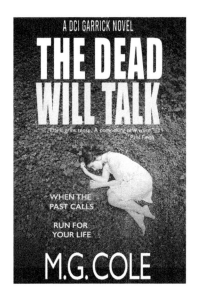

DEAD MAN'S GAME

DCI Garrick 4

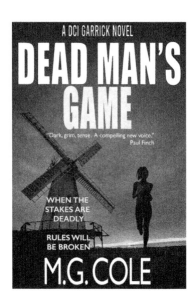

CLEANSING FIRES

DCI Garrick 5

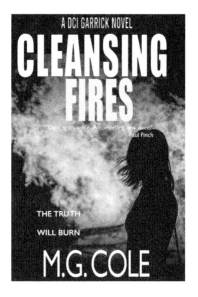

A MURDER OF LIES

DCI Garrick 7 - COMING SOON!

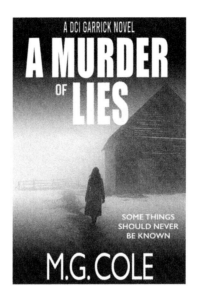

Printed in Great Britain
by Amazon

36599237R00126